If Heaven Touches Earth...

To Jan —
With love and best wishes...
Brenda

If Heaven Touches Earth...
STORIES OF CHRISTMAS

Brenda S. Loux

If Heaven Touches Earth: Stories of Christmas
Copyright © 2016 by Brenda S. Loux
All rights reserved.
Printed by CreateSpace, An Amazon.com Company

ISBN: 978-1-5407-4606-1

Design by Brenda Loux.
Cover image used under license from Shutterstock.com.

www.CreateSpace.com/6747630

For Betty J. Webber

CONTENTS

ACKNOWLEDGMENTS

These stories first appeared as annual Christmas greetings sent to family and friends, and this collection owes its existence to the people who said, in one way or another, "You should put your stories in a book!" The person who said this first, and kept saying it, was my dear friend Betty Webber. She left us too soon to receive her signed copy, but every page is a tribute to her enthusiasm and encouragement.

I am grateful to Carolyn Potser, my high school English composition teacher, for planting seeds of both structure and inspiration. They are still growing.

Finally, a lifetime of appreciation to my parents, Ralph and Millie Loux. They read to me when I was small and helped me learn to read, thereby opening the door to many worlds.

STAR

Kallai loved the stars. Almost every night, before she lay down to sleep, she slipped out of the tent she shared with her sisters, into the desert night. Wrapped in her cloak, sitting on a rock that still held some of the sun's warmth, she gazed up into the twinkling dark. It was beautiful.

One night, Kallai noticed something different. There was a new star, she was sure of it. Brighter than most, it hadn't marched across the sky the way many bright stars did. It was just there. "I'll ask Papa in the morning," she said. "He will tell me about the new star."

The next morning, after helping her mother and sisters make the day's bread, Kallai went looking for her father. She found him with the goats. "Ah, my little one," he said, kissing the top of her head. "What brings you to me so early today? Does Mama need a goat for our dinner?"

"No, Papa, I just want to know something." And she explained to him about the new star.

Papa listened and smiled. "My little star-gazer... there are men who are wiser than I am about the stars. Now if you want to know about the camels or these goats... *that* I can tell you. But about your new star... I don't know." He thought for a moment. "But why should the stars not make more stars, like our goats make more goats?"

Kallai skipped away. But she wondered why the stars would make a grown-up star and not a baby one like the goats did.

For many nights, Kallai watched the new star. She wondered if one day it would go away as quickly as it had come.

One morning, Kallai went to the well to draw water, and as she let her jug down into the well, she heard an unusual noise. She looked all around. Nothing. Kallai pulled the jug up and started back to the tent. Then it came again. Bells. Very faint, but definitely bells. Kallai searched the horizon, but saw nothing. She stood still, listening and watching. Bells, again... and then, far in the distance, something moving. A camel's head... then neck... then what looked like a small caravan. The bells, of course, were on the camels' harnesses.

Kallai put her jug on the ground and ran as fast as she could. She burst into the tent. "Mama! Mama! Camels are coming, this way, they're coming! I heard bells and I looked and looked and then I saw them and I put down my jug and ran and..."

"Child, child! Not so fast," Mama said. "Stop and tell me properly." Kallai took her mother's hand and led her outside. She pointed to the caravan, now shimmering in the distance. "See, Mama!" Her mother shouted to one of Kallai's brothers. "Bani, run and tell your father!"

Papa and the older brothers walked across the desert to meet the caravan. The camels stopped, and the riders dismounted. There was much bowing and waving of hands. Soon, Bani ran back to them, out of breath. They all asked him questions at once. "Hush!" Mama said. "Let him speak!"

Bani panted, "We can't understand one word they say, and they don't understand us, either. But they come in peace. And Papa says there will be a feast tonight!"

Instantly, Mama began giving orders, and everyone scrambled in all directions, eager to do their part to prepare a feast for the unknown visitors. As she worked, Kallai kept an eye on these men in fine robes, covered with the dust of a long journey. Finally, late in the afternoon, everything was ready.

Kallai could not remember such a feast as this. As they all sat around the fire afterwards, the visitors shared delicious dried fruit from their bags, fruit that Kallai had never seen before. Her brothers and sisters brought out instruments, playing and singing for their guests. Then the servants from the caravan took their turn. Even though she could not understand their words, Kallai clapped and danced just the same.

Darkness fell and the stars shone like jewels. Kallai found her father and happily settled in his lap, looking up at her stars. Then she noticed that the visitors were talking among themselves and pointing at the sky. In fact, they were pointing in the direction of her new star.

"Papa," she whispered, "I think they are pointing at my new star."

"What are you saying, little one?"

"My new star, Papa, remember? I asked you about it while you were with the goats."

Papa looked at Kallai and then at the men. There was a smile in his eyes. "Come, we will ask them," he said. Hand in hand, they slowly approached the visitors. Papa bowed. "Honored guests, excuse me. My daughter, this little one, loves the stars. Every night she watches them. Then one day she comes to me and tells me of a new star — she will show you where." Kallai pointed. The men followed her finger and nodded. "She would be most pleased if you tell her the story of this star."

The visitors looked at each other, and one of them stepped forward. He bent down next to Kallai. She watched him intently. The music of his deep voice carried the story along, shaped by his hands and alive in his eyes.

"We have traveled many days," he began. "Our home is far to the east. We all watch the stars and study them and read about them. We, too, saw this new star appear, and we believe it announces the birth of a king." At this, he drew in the sand a stick figure with a crown. "This king would be only a baby." He cradled an imaginary infant in his arms and pointed to the king in the sand. "The star is showing us the way to find this king. We are bringing gifts and we hope to bow down to him one day. Then our journey will be complete."

There was silence in the desert, except for the crackling of the fire. Then Papa spoke softly. "We wish you well on your noble journey. We will not forget this day and the story you have told us. Thank you."

"Thank you," whispered Kallai.

Very early the next morning, as the horizon was just beginning to glow, Kallai awoke to the sounds of camels and men. The caravan was leaving. She remembered the circle of firelight and the story of the star and the baby king. Kallai reached under her blanket and pulled out a tiny doll made of leather and wool. She slipped out of the tent and ran across the sand to the caravan.

In the torchlight, Kallai found the man who told the story, loading bags onto a cranky camel. She stood by shyly, waiting to be noticed. Finally he turned around. "What is it, child?"

Kallai rocked an imaginary baby in her arms, and then put the little doll into his hands. "For the baby king," she said.

The hush of dawn spread across the desert. Understanding softened the man's weathered face. He nodded, kissed the doll, and tucked it carefully into his bag.

VISITOR

It was the first snowstorm, an early one. I put on my coat and boots and walked squinting through the flakes to the end of the driveway. I poked around under the bushes, where the newspaper always lands when thrown from a truck at 35 mph. No paper. I checked the other side of the driveway, in case the laws of physics had been suspended for a day. Nothing there, either. As I stood up, a clump of snow fell from a branch onto my collar.

"#?!*@," I said, and only succeeded in brushing it further into my coat.

Back on the porch, stamping and shaking off the snow, I caught my reflection in the window. I looked closer and then spun around. Standing in the yard behind me was a person in a hooded cloak. The dark green wool was covered with snow, and it was impossible to see who was inside.

"Hello?" I asked.

"Hello, miss," came from inside the hood.

At a loss, I stated the obvious. "Quite a snowstorm, isn't it?"

The stranger took a tentative step towards me. "Indeed it is. I've seen nothing like it."

A woman's voice, with an accent I couldn't place. She pushed the hood back a bit, and I could see blue eyes and brown hair.

Following a split second of mental debate, I threw caution

to the wind and decided to do the hospitable thing, risking a scolding by well-meaning friends.

"Would you like to come inside and get out of this snow? I just put water on for tea."

"Oh, yes, I'd like that very much."

She stepped onto the porch and tried to shake the snow from her cloak. I held the door open and she followed me into the kitchen, her eyes taking in every detail. The kettle was already singing. I turned it off, poured the water, and put some scones into a basket.

My books and papers had taken over the kitchen table, and I tried to herd them to one side.

"Please," I said, motioning to a chair, "sit down."

"Thank you for inviting me in."

"My pleasure," I replied.

We ate and drank in silence for several minutes. Then she pointed to the unruly pile of scribbled papers on the table and asked, "What is all this writing?"

"Well... it's my Christmas card. But it's not finished. For... oh, I don't know how many years... instead of buying cards, I write something." I stopped and frowned. "No, that's not really how it happens. A story knocks at the door and I let it in and watch what happens and write it down. I don't know if that makes sense, but... I can't say that it comes from me."

I glanced up. She was listening, and nodded.

"Stories are a gift," she said. "They are bigger than the one who writes them down."

I smiled. "Yes."

Outside, a big blue jay perched on the red maple tree, cracking a sunflower seed. I fetched the kettle and refilled our cups.

"What are these... these... hanging things?" she asked, looking around the kitchen.

"You mean the Christmas decorations?" I asked, not quite understanding. Anyone could see they were Christmas decorations.

"Tell me, please... what is this... Christmas?"

My face must have betrayed disbelief. How can any person in America in December not know about Christmas?! But she was obviously sincere. I thought for a minute.

"Come, I will show you," and I went into the living room and turned on the Christmas tree lights.

"See... look at this." I pointed to the small wooden nativity scene under the tree. "This is a picture of a story that happened long ago. God... the great King of the universe... became small, a baby, to visit the earth." I picked up the tiny baby Jesus and put it in her hand.

"He came to be with us, as one of us. And his life redeems all of creation from darkness. This coming of the King... this is Christmas."

She knelt down and looked at the figures. "I know this visit," she said softly. "It echoed in the heavens."

Snow blew against the windowpane like grains of sand. The wind paused to catch its breath, and mystery almost came to rest.

But like a summons from the world of clocks and calendars, the phone rang.

"Excuse me," I said, and went into the other room to answer it.

"Hello?... I already get the paper delivered... yes, Thursday, Friday, and Sunday... But I don't want the other days... Yeah, I know it's free, but I wouldn't have time to read it... thanks anyway."

I came back into the kitchen. "Doggone it, I should've told him I didn't get my..." I stopped in mid-sentence and looked around. I was alone.

Forgetting boots, I stepped outside onto the porch and scanned the snow for footprints. There were none. The chill soon penetrated my wool socks and I went back inside.

There was a small wet spot on the floor where the snowy cloak had been. And on the table, between two lukewarm cups of tea, was the baby Jesus.

ELIZABETH

Everyone laughed when they heard the news, and who can blame them? Why, I've laughed myself, many times! Who could believe it... *me*, Elizabeth, the one everyone thought was too old to have a baby, holding this child in my arms... *my* child!

And yet, in a way I don't completely understand, I feel he's not really my child. Oh, I gave birth to him, of course. But the fact that he was born at all is a gift from God, and I am convinced that, even now, God has claimed his life.

And such a precious little life it is, as I hold him and see these tiny fingers and toes... see that smile and hear his cries... and judging from those loud cries, I wonder what sort of voice he will have when he is a man! Hmm, I wonder... will I even be alive to hear it?

My husband Zechariah's voice was taken away in the months before the baby was born. He couldn't speak, not a word, because... Do you have time to hear the whole story? I never tire of telling it, but you should sit down.

Zechariah is a priest, and one day he was chosen to burn incense in the temple. All the people were outside praying and waiting for him. They waited for a long time, wondering, and then worrying that he was taking so long. When he finally did come out, he couldn't speak!

You see, while Zechariah was in the temple, an angel appeared to him, right there next to the altar. He was terrified, as anyone would be. But the angel said:

> *Do not be afraid, Zechariah; your prayer has been heard. Your wife Elizabeth will bear you a son, and you are to give him the name John. He will be a joy and delight to you, and many will rejoice because of his birth, for he will be great in the sight of the Lord.*

Zechariah was a bit skeptical and asked the angel how he could be sure of this, since we are both old. Looking back, he'd tell you now that asking questions wasn't the best idea. But I get chills when I think of the angel's reply:

> *I am Gabriel. I stand in the presence of God, and I have been sent to speak to you and to tell you this good news. And now you will be silent and not able to speak until the day this happens, because you did not believe my words, which will come true at their proper time.*

Well, it was very quiet in this house for all those months. And at the proper time the angel's words *did* come true, as you can see by this little one. He has been such a joy to us, in just these few weeks. Such a change in our life! But wait, there's more to the story...

Before my son was born, I had an unexpected visit from my dear cousin Mary. The moment I heard her greeting as she entered our house, I felt the baby jump for joy. I listened with joy and wonder as she told me that she, too, was visited by an angel! She remembered every word the angel said:

> *Do not be afraid, Mary, you have found favor with God. You will be with child and give birth to a son, and you are to give him the name Jesus. He will be great and will be called the Son of the Most High... his kingdom will never end.*

And most amazing, the angel made it clear that the child

would be conceived by the power of God alone! *"For nothing is impossible with God,"* were the angel's last words.

Oh, I wonder…these miracles…this angel, Gabriel, who stands in the presence of God! Every day I wonder, what will the future bring for Mary's son and my son?

Mary stayed with me for about three months, and not long after she left, our son was born. You have never seen such a celebration among our friends and relatives as there was that day! When the time came for the baby to be named, everyone assumed he would be called Zechariah, after his father. I had to speak up and say "No! He is to be called John."

That caused a good deal of confusion, of course, because no one in our family is named John. So they looked to Zechariah for an answer, and he asked for a tablet. In big letters he wrote, "His name is John!"

And at that moment, my husband could speak. Oh, it was good to hear his voice again! He began to praise God with words that were like a song, and at the end, holding little John in his arms, he said:

> *And you, little child, will be called the prophet of the Most High; for you will go before the Lord to prepare the way for his coming. It will be for you to give his people knowledge of their salvation through the forgiveness of their sins.*
>
> *Because the heart of our God is full of mercy towards us, the first light of Heaven shall come to visit us — to shine on those who lie in darkness and under the shadow of death, and to guide our feet into the path of peace.*

After I heard those words, I felt my heart would burst. Tears ran down my face and dripped onto baby John. I can't tell you what it all means. All I know is that, somehow, God is coming to be with us, to be our light in this darkness.

TEACAKES

The St. Davids train station was deserted. I dropped four quarters in the per-day slot for space 17 and walked through the underpass to the inbound side of the tracks. My footsteps clunked on the steep wooden stairs to the platform.

A cold, heavy mist hung on the early-morning darkness, slowing the minutes to a crawl. On the opposite platform, a silent holiday chorus of posters sang the praises of iPod. Just as I began to suspect that I was the only person alive in St. Davids, a man with a laptop bag slung over his shoulder appeared, bought a newspaper from the box, and started reading. In keeping with standard commuter etiquette, we did not acknowledge each other's existence.

I stared down the tracks. The glow around the bend announced the arrival of the 5:35 R5. It was silent at that distance, but as it rumbled, clanked and hissed into the station, it wasn't hard to imagine that behind the blinding headlight was an old steam engine. I hoisted myself up the steps and walked toward the front of the train.

"Tickets, please! All tickets!" The conductor swayed down the aisle.

"Round trip to 30th Street, please. Off-peak return."

"Eight twenty-five." He peeled my change from his wad of bills and fished three quarters from a pocket that sounded like a slot machine jackpot. There was a flurry of hole-punching. "Don't lose that, it's your return ticket."

It's easy to fall asleep on a train, especially when the windows are dirty and you have nothing to worry about. I knew I'd have plenty of time at 30th Street to collect my Amtrak tickets, eat breakfast, and get a nice big cup of coffee for the ride to Washington. I pulled the D.C. map from my backpack for one last check. With a brisk walk down Massachusetts Avenue, I'd make it to the convention center by 9:00 for the seminar.

I slouched down in my seat. From somewhere in the back, I could hear the conductor shouting the stops. "Villanova!" "Rosemont!" "Bryn Mawr!" But he kept getting farther away, and I don't remember anything past Ardmore.

◅ — ▻

I was jolted out of my dream by a loud voice, but the words didn't register at first. "Center City! Reading Terminal, downtown Philadelphia!" The train was empty. I grabbed my backpack and raced to the door, down the steps, and onto the platform. I looked around, stunned. It was familiar, but wrong. Very wrong. It was Reading Terminal. Not the Market it's been for almost 20 years, but a train station again. I stared in every direction, an island in the stream of passengers heading for their trains.

I wandered into the station and sat on a bench near the shoeshine boys, dimly aware of the swirl of activity. After a few minutes, I looked at everyone more closely. They looked like people you see in old family photos... your grandparents when they were 30, for example. But something wasn't quite right. I kept watching. And then I realized what it was. These people were in color, not black and white.

I stood up and looked around for a newsstand. Across the station was a vendor, and I walked over to scan the banner of the *Philadelphia Inquirer*. Monday, December 20, 1943. All of a sudden the walls seemed to be closing in, and I hurried outside.

Market Street was filled with pedestrians and cars, and I was swept along by the crowd. I joined a cluster of shoppers admiring the holiday displays in the window of Wanamaker's, and for a very few seconds I forgot about being in the wrong decade. But the smell of coffee brought me back to... what, *reality?*... and I realized how hungry I was.

There was a small bakery halfway down the block. I held the door for the folks coming out, amid thank yous, Merry Christmases, and tipping of hats. I had one foot in the door when it hit me. *My money is 60 years too new.* I backed out and stood on the sidewalk. As I watched the people passing by, it was obvious that I stood out like color in a black and white photo. Jeans, hiking shoes, Polartec jacket and gloves, a backpack, and no fashionable hat. *If I go in there, they'll probably throw me out, never mind the money.* But I was hungry. I pulled a dollar from my wallet and wadded it up with some change in my pocket. I told myself that a friendly smile is probably a good idea in any decade, and with a deep breath and a growl in my stomach, I stepped inside.

The aroma of bread and baked goods spoke a warm welcome, but the woman behind the counter was a bit skeptical of the new customer. "Yes?" she asked. I figured the quicker the transaction, the better it would be for all concerned.

"Good morning!" I jumped right in. "It's hard to decide, everything looks wonderful." She softened around the edges, just a bit. "Let's see... may I have two of those rolls, and... what are these cookies in the front?"

"They are Russian teacakes."

"Half a dozen of those, also."

She bagged my purchase. "Fifteen cents, please."

I handed her a quarter and asked, "Do you only make the Russian teacakes at Christmas?"

"Yes, they are an old recipe, only for the holidays."

As I hoped, she took the money without examination and returned my change. "Thank you very much. Merry Christmas!" And I escaped out the door.

I worked my way back to Reading Terminal, dodging shoppers who could barely see from behind their stacks of boxes. I sat on a bench and took a roll from the bag. It was still warm. *Now what?* I stared at the train board listing departures, and saw Quakertown. My hometown in 1943. Now there's a chance you don't get every day. I debated the merits of a visit, but how do you apply logic in a situation that defies it? I walked to the ticket counter.

"Hello. Quakertown, please." The agent looked over his glasses at me.

"One-way or round-trip?" Now there was a good question.

"Uhhh... one-way."

"One dollar and twenty-five cents." I pulled the crumpled dollar and a quarter from my pocket.

"How long is that ride?" I asked, trying the diversionary tactic again.

"Let's see... little over an hour, I believe." He handed me the ticket. "Track 3, leaves in 10 minutes."

It was just starting to snow as I walked out to the tracks. Passengers were boarding, and I took a seat in the last car. After a few minutes, the engine rumbled and the train slowly pulled away from the station. You can't make a plan of action when you have no business being where you are in the first place, so I just looked out the window at the snow and the few small towns. After about an hour, the whistle sounded at the first railroad crossing in Quakertown.

The train hissed and squealed to a halt at the station. I slowly descended the steps and looked around, half-afraid it would all disappear and leave me alone in the snow.

"Excuse me, miss... you're lookin' a bit lost. Will someone be comin' to pick you up or can I give you a ride somewheres?" The friendly voice came from an old Chevy pickup truck, and I squinted against the snow, peering in at the old man in overalls.

"Oh, thank you, sir... but I'm in town... ahhh... sort of by surprise... visiting relatives. I'll be walking, I think."

"Not such a good day for that. And who might your relatives be?"

"Well, the Maugles up on Main Street, and Herstines over on Thatcher Road."

"Yep, yep, I know them both. Well, you tell them all Merry Christmas."

"Thank you… and the same to you." The idea of speaking to my relatives seemed somehow out of bounds, so I decided I wouldn't seek out the opportunity. Just thinking of how to explain who I was made my head spin.

The pickup sputtered off and I pulled my hood up and headed down Broad Street. I looked in at Klein's store. Miss Klein was there, easily recognizable with her bright red lipstick, surrounded by a multitude of items that couldn't be found anywhere else in town or possibly the universe. A bit farther down the block was Cassel's grocery store where, in years to come, I would be fascinated by the array of cereal boxes.

For hours, I wandered around town like a ghost. I looked in the back window of Fritz's Bakery on Hellertown Avenue. There was Grandpop Herstine, dusted with flour and looking very young, running loaf after loaf of bread through the slicing machine. I walked all the way out to Thatcher Road, where Mom and her sisters, Jane and Anna, ran home from the one-room schoolhouse and huddled around the coal stove in the front room to dry off and warm up. I could hear them singing Christmas carols. On 9th Street, my great-grandfather tended to a sea of startlingly red poinsettias in the greenhouses behind Haring's flower shop. At 1404 Broad Street, Pop-Pop shoveled the sidewalk and threw snowballs at Dad and his uncle Clyde as they sledded down 14th Street. Uncle Willie swept off the porch at Nanny's house on Main Street when he got home from work, and through the front window I saw Grammy and Nanny in the living room, talking and laughing as they arranged Christmas decorations.

Daylight faded. I wandered in the direction of the train

station, a few warm tears mixing with melting snowflakes on my face. Scenes from the day played through my mind, like family photos come to life. It was a gift, this falling into the past. But a gift that could only be enjoyed from the other side of the window.

I couldn't think of anything else to do but take the train back to Philadelphia, so I bought a ticket. I was exhausted from walking in the snow all day, and hungry. When the train arrived, I slumped into a seat and pulled a roll from the bakery bag in my backpack. It was well-chilled from spending the day outdoors, but delicious beyond all expectation. I leaned against the window, closed my eyes, and slipped under the blanket of sleep.

⤝——⤞

The opening notes of Beethoven's Fifth Symphony from a cell phone penetrated my consciousness, but just barely. Then a man's voice. "Hello? Yeah, I'm just getting to the station. I'll be there in 15 minutes... Did he bring the contract? Good. I'll be there soon."

I opened my eyes to the familiar left-hand curve of the tracks as the R5 approaches 30th Street Station. I was thoroughly dazed, like when the alarm clock yanks you out of a dream. I picked up the ticket receipt and what I could find of my wits and joined the line of passengers filing down the aisle. Inside the station, I headed straight for the Amtrak ticket machines, swiped my credit card, and waited for the tickets to print. It was all so normal, but I couldn't quite believe it. What I really wanted was to hear a familiar voice, but the explanation for a 6:30 a.m. phone call would have to make more sense than "I need confirmation that I'm in the right decade."

I circled the station shops, consuming my weekly allowance of cholesterol at McDonald's for breakfast, then picked up a bagel and big cup of coffee for the train ride to D.C. A line of people waiting to board Amtrak's 7:05 Metroliner snaked through the station, and I shuffled along in my place. Once aboard, I settled into the comfortable seat and pulled out my phone. I listened to the ring at Mom and Dad's house, hope tinged with fear.

"Hi Dad! Did I wake you up? No? OK, good. I told you and Mom I was going to Washington today for work, right?... Yeah, I'm actually on the train now... OK, I just wanted to be sure. Have a good day... Love you... Bye."

The warmth of home settled like a down comforter as I sipped the coffee. *Two hours with nothing to do but read. What could be better?* I reached into my backpack for a book... and pulled out the bag of Russian teacakes.

STABLE

Most of the time, I don't even notice the folks who come to the inn. I guess they all look the same to me, just dusty strangers who disappear in the morning. Besides, if I don't keep to my work, I'll catch it from my master, and I don't look for that kind of trouble. There's no pleasing him, even on a good day.

Carrying water back from the well late in the afternoon, I see these two at the door of the inn. The man, he looks worried. And when you see the girl... well, you know why he's worried, because she's pregnant out to here! She just might have that baby while they're standing there at the door. I'm sixteen now, and she can't be older than I am.

The man is speaking to my master. I can't hear what he's saying, but I know well enough he's asking for a room — just like all the others parading through town this week on account of that worthless census. Now my master is a lot of things, but quiet's not one of them. So before the man is done speaking, he's bellowing like an ox, "I'm tellin' you, I got no rooms! You seen all the people on the road, didn't you? Well, they all stopped here for the night! I got nothin' left!"

That's all I hear, as I carry water back to the stable for the animals. About the only peaceful minute I get in a day is watering those animals, so I don't hurry, if you know what I mean. While I'm busy in the stable, the door opens, and I figure it's my master coming to find out what's taking so long. It's him, all right, but not alone. He's got those two with him, and he says, "Here it is, and like I told you, if you want it, it'll cost you the same as a room."

That man could get blood from a turnip, everybody says, and there isn't anybody that squeezes harder than he does. But the stranger just says, "Agreed," and gives him the coins. My master takes the money and leaves them standing there. I look up for a second because I can't believe even he would take money to let a pregnant girl sleep with the cows... but I look away from their eyes because I'm ashamed, even though it's not my idea. I finish with the animals and get out of there quick.

Where I sleep is out back, in the building next to the stable. Sometime in the middle of the night, I wake up. No birds or roosters are making a racket, so I roll over to go back to sleep. But then I hear a sound, and now I'm awake, sure enough. I know that sound. It's the girl in the stable, she's having that baby right now.

I lay still for a minute and think of the beating I'll get if my master finds out I'm interfering with the paid customers. I don't care.

I get up quiet as can be and go outside. There's no light, just the stars and a little slice of moon. But I can see well enough, and I go to the back door of the inn, holding my breath and stalking around like a cat. I find a lamp and an armful of rags, and I take them out to the stable.

The door is open just a crack and I say "Hello?" real soft. Right away the man comes over. I whisper, "I brought you some rags and a lamp."

"Can you get water?" he asks. So back I go to the inn and draw water out of the big pots in the back room. Still no sign of anyone else awake, lucky for me. I carry the water back to the stable and then go off to a dark corner while they tend to the baby. I don't like to leave, thinking they might need something else. But I don't like to stay where I don't belong, either.

After a while the man comes over to my corner. "Would you like to see the baby?" Well of course I would, so I follow him over to the girl. The baby is all wrapped up in those rags. "Boy or girl?" I ask, because I can't tell. "Boy," they both say at the same time. The girl's holding him close, and I know the strongest man in the world couldn't take that baby away from her.

But she's exhausted. I look around and wonder where they can lay the baby so she can get some sleep. The man must be thinking the same thing, because he gathers up the cleanest straw he can find and fills the feed box with it. Then he comes over to the girl and kneels down next to her. The girl gives the baby a kiss and puts him in the man's arms. He's in no hurry to put that baby down, but finally he lays him in the straw, real careful.

We all sit there quiet for a time, just watching the baby. Then the man says, "Thanks for helping us. I know it's risky for you to do it." And the girl reaches out and takes my hand. I'm not used to folks taking notice of me in a good way, so I don't know what to say. I think for a minute. "He's a beautiful baby. He'll grow up and make you proud of him." They both smile, but they're heavy with tiredness, and something else I can't put a name to.

Just then, there are footsteps outside shuffling around, and men's voices, excited but quiet. The girl squeezes my hand without meaning to. There's a very soft knock. The man reaches for his staff and goes to the door. He braces himself and opens it just a crack. "What do you want?" he says, none too friendly. A handful of voices whisper an answer, then silence. The man hesitates, then he steps back and opens the door.

In come the men and boys who tend the sheep outside town, all out of breath and soaking wet with sweat as if they ran the whole way. They look... well, scared half to death, if you really want to know. But when they see the baby, their eyes light up like they just found buried treasure. And the whole lot of them, smelly and caked with mud, kneel down in front of the baby!

For the life of me, I can't figure out what's going on, but there they stayed, with their faces to the ground, for a good long while.

After a time, they look up. And one of them, the oldest of the bunch, all wrinkled with sun and wind, takes a deep breath and swallows the lump in his throat. The others nod at him to go ahead.

It started out like a regular night, he says, most of the sheep asleep, all quiet. But then the dark exploded with light and an angel stood there with them, shining with the very glory of heaven! He can't understand how they all didn't just die on the spot from fear. But the angel gave a message... now here they all put in their bit to be sure he has every word just right...

"Don't be afraid! Look, I bring you good news of great joy for everyone. This very day, in the town of David, there was born for you a Savior — yes, the Messiah, the Lord! And this is how you will recognize him: You will find a baby wrapped in pieces of cloth and lying in a feeding trough." Then the armies of heaven filled the sky, praising God. "Glory to God in the highest heaven! Peace on earth among people of good will!"

A sound like nothing you've ever heard, he says. Tears stream down his face, and I know he hears it still.

I get down on my knees next to the baby. He's asleep. This night is more than I can understand. But I know that somehow, on account of this baby, the dividing line between heaven and earth has been rubbed out.

CABIN

The rain blew sideways as I crossed the parking lot, and the early December darkness hung like a cold, soggy blanket. I fumbled with the car key, opened the door, and collapsed, awkward and dripping, into the driver's seat, still holding my lunch cooler and briefcase. I was dazed. Working late was only part of it. I was still suffering the effects of my ill-advised trip to the mall at lunchtime.

I just needed one gift, the Pollyanna for a random co-worker drawn from a hat. I envisioned a quick-strike, precision operation... *The Polar Express* DVD plucked from the rack at Sam Goody and back at my desk in 45 minutes. I might have succeeded, but for the fact that every Corporate American within five miles of the mall took an early lunch to join me. Weaving my way through Sears to avoid gridlock, I nearly got sucked into a live demo of the Roomba Robotic Vacuum. But I tore myself away and managed to run the gauntlet of cosmetics without getting spritzed by the latest from Estée Lauder. I elbowed into position at Sam Goody, snatched the DVD, and waited in line behind the person returning three items, buying ten, and paying with store credit, various gift certificates, and an expired credit card. I was back at my desk in just under two hours.

Now, exhaling for what felt like the first time since lunch, I started the engine and pulled out of the parking lot. The temperature display read 44 degrees. The back roads that provide lovely vistas of stone farmhouses and horse farms by day become a twisting maze of blind corners and magically appearing deer by night. I drove slowly into the pocket of light ahead. The rain drummed on the roof and blended with soft Christmas music from the stereo as I climbed Union Hill Road to the stop sign. There I came upon three deer in a quandary about whether or not to cross. They eventually thought better of it and turned with a graceful leap back into the darkness. I wound my way down the steep descent, past the falling-down barn, to the imposing stone overpass of the unused railroad. I paused and then passed through the one-lane opening.

Humming in harmony to the music, I drove unconsciously for a few minutes. And then, dimly at first, I realized that something was wrong. Or at least different. The road was no longer asphalt. It was gravel. I had not come to Route 29, as I should have. The rain was gone. Instead, the air swirled with flakes, like a snow globe. I glanced at the display. 28 degrees. Puzzled, I slowed down. There was a faint glow up ahead, and soon I came to a small log house. Smoke curled from a stone chimney, and soft light shone through curtained windows. The road ended in front of the house. I turned off the engine and all was quiet.

After a moment, the door opened and a bearded face peered out. I opened the car door and stood with one foot out and one foot in.

"Evening!" a voice called.

"Hello," I answered with much less enthusiasm.

"So you're lost, then," he said.

"Well, I didn't think I was, but... seeing as I don't know how I got here..."

"Yep, yep, and you're not the first. You'll come in, then." It was more a statement than an invitation, but welcoming, nonetheless.

I walked through the snow to the porch, as he held the door open. His galoshes were unbuckled, as if he had just slipped them on but didn't intend to go anywhere. His red flannel shirt and denim jeans were well worn, and his hair and beard were grey. He had bright eyes, like an Irish storyteller.

He left his boots at the door, and I did the same with my shoes. The floor, walls, and ceiling were all of cedar, and there was a stone fireplace along one wall. Two cats lay on a rug in front of the fire, and each opened one disinterested eye to judge whether or not the intruder posed any threat. Around a corner at the far end of the room was the kitchen, and the smell of baking bread was unmistakable and nearly intoxicating.

"Here, let's take your wet things over by the fire to dry," he said, and I handed him my coat and gloves. I stood uncertainly by the door. Just then a woman came from the kitchen, wiping her hands on a towel. "It's so good that you found us tonight," she said, smiling. This seemed an odd greeting, but they both were so pleasant and full of life that I could only muster the slightest uneasiness.

"Let's sit down for a bit, and that bread will be ready in just a few minutes. Will you have some hot chocolate?"

"Yes, please," I replied. We all sank into the chairs in front of the fire.

"Not many people find their way here," the man said. "But those that do, they all got that same look in their eyes just like you."

"How do you mean?" I asked.

"Like half of you is somewhere else," he said. "The better half, if you know what I mean."

I smiled ruefully. "Yeah, I know." And I told them in more detail than necessary about my lunchtime trip to the mall, how busy I was at work, that there was no time to get things done around the house, and how the Christmas season so often feels like a bobsled with no brakes.

They smiled and nodded at my monologue, but I suspected they'd never been to the mall. For a time we all just watched the fire. The logs crackled and hissed, and sparks flew upward when one broke apart. The cats slept on the hearth, snow fluttered against the windows, and somewhere a clock ticked. I felt the bobsled lose momentum.

The mantle was covered with holly and evergreen branches, and in the center was a wooden Christmas tree, carved from a log. I stood up to have a better look. Hanging from its snow-laden branches were tiny wooden ornaments, no two the same, and each one carefully crafted. There was a holly leaf with berries, a snowflake, pine cone, bear, rolling pin, mittens, cookie cutter, manger, a variety of woodworking tools, a sheep, teapot, sled, and a twelve-pointed star. I'd never seen anything like it.

"You made this?" I asked.

"Well, the carving part," he chuckled. "I can't take credit for the wood." He joined me in front of the fireplace, sidestepping the cats.

"The star is my favorite," I said, pointing to its place at the top of the tree. He gently unhooked it and put it in my hand.

"That one's special to me, too." And then he was thinking out loud. "We all lose our way now and then. Comes from not seeing. Nothing like a sky full of stars to set us right again."

"Amen," I said, and carefully placed the star back at the top of the tree.

The woman got up and went to the kitchen, soon calling for us to join her. A steaming loaf of whole wheat bread was cut into thick slices, surrounded by butter, honey, and raspberry jam. Mugs of hot chocolate all around. We sat at the table and the man bowed his head. "Father of the heavenly lights, for these and all blessings, we give thanks." We all three said, "Amen."

There wasn't much need for talk. The shared enjoyment of food and company was enough. The cats awoke from their slumber to see if there might be something for them. There was, a plate of milk on the floor. I drained the last drop of hot chocolate and listened to the soft lapping of the cats.

I looked at my hosts and smiled. "Thank you."

Their eyes twinkled. "It's our pleasure," the woman said. "Truly it is."

We all stood up from the table and the man went to fetch my coat from the chair by the fireplace. The woman walked me to the door. I pulled on my shoes, the man helped with my coat, and I stepped out into the gently falling snow. I turned to wave before climbing into the car. The sound of the engine was foreign, and I backed around and headed up the gravel road. The glow of the cabin quickly faded from the rear-view mirror, and soon the railroad overpass appeared in the headlights. I paused and drove through. Rain pounded on the roof, and I could see the stop sign at Route 29.

In a few minutes I was home. I walked to the end of the driveway and pulled a handful of Christmas cards and marketing debris from the mailbox. It was good to be in the house and out of the rain, and I spent the evening baking cookies and enjoying the Christmas tree lights. It seemed the perfect night to read *A Child's Christmas in Wales*, and so I did.

Next morning, I packed up some of the cookies to take to work. The reality of my visit to the cabin had started to crumble around the edges, but the runaway bobsled was still gone, and I didn't miss it. I drove to work along my usual route, paying special attention to the railroad overpass. Needless to say, there was no gravel road.

Work was the usual blur of activity punctuated by looming crises, but I was determined to leave on time. So at 4:00, I shut down the computer, gathered up my bags, and put on my coat. I reached into the pocket for car keys... and found the twelve-pointed star.

KINGDOM

Oil lamps flickered in the dimly lit room, and the soft sounds of twilight floated through the open windows. Muffled voices of children playing, camels and other livestock settling down, and the faraway howl of a jackal. The nearly-full moon pushed above the horizon, sending a stream of silver light into the room.

Alazar paused at the doorway. His eyes scanned the shadowy figures clustered in twos and threes, then focused on the far corner of the room. He moved slowly through the low murmurs of hushed voices.

An old man lay on a bed in the corner, eyes closed and chest rising and falling with shallow breaths. Alazar knelt by his side and took his hand. "Papa," he said softly. "It's Alazar. I'm here." He felt the slightest pressure on his hand. It was a far cry from his grandfather's iron grip as a younger man, but Alazar gave thanks for this last, frail connection with his hero.

A caravan of memories wandered through Alazar's mind, timeless moments gathered by an unseen hand. He closed his eyes, drawn into that stream of life, until a gentle hand on his shoulder brought him back.

Alazar stood up and put his arms around his grandmother. "He thinks the world of you," she whispered. Alazar's eyes filled with tears, and he nodded. His grandmother sat down next to

Papa, and Alazar made his way slowly out into the night. The piercing moonlight cast shadows across his path as he walked through the garden to his grandfather's favorite fig tree. He sat on a bench and buried his face in his hands.

For as long as Alazar could remember, his grandfather talked about the baby king. Not long before Alazar was born, his grandfather and the other sky-watchers saw a king's star. They followed it for hundreds of miles across the desert, carrying gifts to honor the king when they found him.

As a boy, Alazar loved to hear about the wild animals and bandits and a host of other dangers that his grandfather and companions outsmarted or outfought on their journey. But it was plain that all those adventures meant very little to his grandfather. Every time Papa told the story, the intensity built as they approached Jerusalem. Even now, in the quiet of the garden, Alazar looked into Papa's eyes, alive with the memory, and heard his voice...

> "So we're close to Jerusalem, and we don't escape notice... asking everyone we meet, *Where is the child born to be king of the Jews?* We tell about seeing his star in the east and coming to pay him honor. The place was in an uproar soon enough, and it didn't take long for news to reach the palace. The king, Herod, sends messengers to invite us to meet him in private. But before we arrive, he finds out from the priests and teachers where this leader is to be born. The village of Bethlehem, in Judah. He tells us this when we meet him, and asks us exactly when the star appeared."
>
> Papa's hands tighten into fists as he pauses. "It makes my skin crawl even now, thinking of that scoundrel. He sends us off to Bethlehem and tells us to search for the child and report back to him when we find him — so he can worship him, too, he says. So we go straight to Bethlehem, and that star leads us to the very house where the

child is! We go into the house and find the baby with his mother, Mary." Papa wipes his eyes.

"To come all that way, following that star, and now to see the baby king…" He shakes his head. "I thought my heart would burst with the joy and wonder of it. We fall to our knees and bow down to him, then open our gifts… incense, gold, myrrh… they were fit for a king."

Papa is silent for a long time, seeing it all again. Then, almost as an afterthought, he says, "They named the baby Jesus. We had dreams warning us not to go back to Herod, so we came home by a different way."

Alazar lifted his head from his hands and looked up at the fig tree. He knew the question that haunted his grandfather's days, woven through the moments and memories. *What became of the baby king?* To be announced in such a way by heaven must herald a kingdom like no other. But for thirty years, no news of it had reached across the desert.

The familiar noises of the night crept back into Alazar's consciousness, but were soon mingled with another sound. From the open windows, voices of grief carried across the garden, women crying. His grandfather was gone. Alazar stared up into the great canopy of stars, and all at once it became clear to him. "I will find your baby king, Papa. I will see if he has a kingdom."

In the next days and weeks, family and friends buried and mourned for Papa. But Alazar's mind was on his quest. He told Tamal, his closest friend. "I will go with you," Tamal said. And so together they made a plan for the journey. One of the servants, Josech, had come back from that land with Alazar's grandfather. They would take him as guide and interpreter.

When all was ready, Alazar told his family. "Many years ago, our Papa followed the star to find the baby king. To honor Papa, I am going to search for this king whose birth was written in the heavens. May God help me and bring me safely back to you."

Early the next morning, long before the sun appeared on the

horizon, Alazar and Tamal loaded the camels, said goodbye to their families, and set off with Josech across the desert. As they traveled day after day, Alazar wondered how closely their path followed his grandfather's.

One morning, after weeks of travel, they rode slowly into a small village. As usual, a cluster of children gathered in their wake. They dismounted and tied up the camels, then found a group of old men sitting in the shade. Josech greeted them.

"You come from a far land," said one of the men.

"Indeed," said Josech. "We hope that you can give us news of a king."

"A king? Well, this is Judah, so you mean King Herod?" A low grumble rose from the circle of men, and one of them spat on the ground. Alazar felt a chill go up his spine as this name took shape again from Papa's story.

"No, sir, Herod is not the king we are in search of." The men exchanged glances and waited for Josech to continue. "The king we're looking for is called Jesus. Born in Bethlehem, about thirty years ago."

Alazar felt the weight of his journey resting on their response, and it almost suffocated him. The men looked at each other, and then several chuckled.

"Well, he's not the king you're after, but there's a teacher called Jesus roaming the countryside these days. Just came through here a day or two ago, headed the same direction you're going. If you stay on the road you'll probably come upon him later today. He doesn't seem to travel very fast."

As Josech relayed the man's reply, the life seeped out of Alazar. He walked back to the camels in silence, and stared for a long time down the road they had just traveled. When he finally spoke, his voice was so soft that the others had to step closer to hear.

"If there was a king called Jesus in this land anytime in the past thirty years, those men would know," he said. "Herod is still in power... maybe he found the baby king even though

Papa and the others didn't return to him." He forced himself to speak the horrible thought. "Maybe he killed the baby."

"It could be so," Tamal said, gripping Alazar's shoulder. "But we have come this far. I say we should continue down the road. Maybe we can hear this teacher Jesus. Maybe we will meet someone who knows more than these men. Don't lose heart, my friend. Our journey is not lost. Not yet."

Alazar nodded, but without much hope. They made the camels ready and continued on. It was mid-afternoon, between villages, when their way was blocked by a crowd of people. "What's going on?" Josech asked a boy nearby.

"It's Jesus, the rabbi," he answered.

They found a place to tie the camels, and stretched to see from the edge of the crowd. The teacher was sitting on a rock, talking. "What is he saying?" Alazar asked.

"He's telling a story," Josech said, then paused. "He's telling about the kingdom of Heaven." Josech frowned and cocked his head to hear better. "He says the kingdom of Heaven is like some treasure which has been buried in a field. A man finds it and buries it again, then goes off overjoyed to sell all his possessions to buy himself that field."

Alazar and Tamal looked at each other, puzzled. "The kingdom — of Heaven?" They watched Jesus as he talked, and Josech translated, story after story. When he was finished speaking, Jesus moved into the crowd, and people pressed close to him... blind, crippled, deranged... bodies and minds out of joint. He spoke to them, touched them...

"No!" Josech exclaimed in horror. "Look, he touches the lepers!" And then...

"Alazar!" Tamal said, fear and wonder in his voice. "Do you see what is happening?"

Alazar couldn't take his eyes from the rabbi. "I see, but it can't be true."

"He's healing them!" Tamal said.

Without looking away, Alazar said, "Josech, find out where the teacher is from."

Josech disappeared into the crowd and returned within minutes. "He's from Nazareth, in Galilee. North of here, north of Jerusalem."

"He may be from there now, but where was he born?" Tamal asked. Josech slipped back into the crowd. "And find out his mother's name!" Alazar called after him. They watched Josech moving from person to person, until he was very close to Jesus. He spoke to a man briefly, then hurried back to them.

"Bethlehem, in Judah. Not far from here." He paused, looking at Alazar. "Mary."

The sights and sounds around Alazar faded away. He stumbled back from the crowd and scrambled up a rocky hill overlooking the people. Tamal and Josech followed him, and for a long time they watched the teacher, and heard the echo of his words…

Ask and it will be given to you. Search and you will find. Knock and the door will be opened for you. The one who asks will always receive; the one who is searching will always find, and the door is opened to the one who knocks.

The sun set, and the horizon glowed with its memory. The people had long since dispersed, and the sky slowly changed from blue to black, filling with stars. Alazar lay on his back and looked up into the endless night.

"Tamal," he asked, "did we find Papa's king today?"

Tamal took a deep breath and exhaled slowly. "What does your heart tell you?"

"My heart is warm, but my head spins," Alazar said. "It's too big for me."

"That it is," said Tamal thoughtfully. "But what should we expect, if heaven touches earth?"

SOLDIER

Riina had never known a Christmas without the shades tightly closed. In her village, it was forbidden to celebrate Christmas, and so they had to keep it like a secret. All the traditions of their people, all the songs, the special food and drink... they took care not to let anything spill out of their own little house. The others in the village did the same, but it was never spoken of, not even in whispers. Because you never knew where trouble might come from.

The day before Christmas, Mama and Riina's older sisters, Maarja and Triinu, were in the kitchen, baking and cooking for the holiday meals. Riina tried to help, but she was in the way more than helping. Then she thought of something special she could do all by herself. She could go to the woods and collect pinecones and branches and holly to decorate the house. She chose one of Papa's pocketknives and found a sack to carry everything home. She put on her coat and hat and boots, and out she went.

It was snowing again. Big flakes fell out of the heavy gray sky and settled on her coat. She noticed how the snow crunched under her boots, and how the birds knocked snow off of branches when they landed. It was not a long walk to the woods, and soon she was gathering pinecones. The next job — cutting branches — was harder. A saw would have been better than a pocketknife. It took all her energy and concentration, and she didn't notice anything else. Until she heard the crunching of footsteps behind her. Someone... or something... big.

She stopped cutting and turned her head. The first thing she saw was boots. Big boots. And a rifle. A military coat and hat. Her heart beat as fast as a little bird's.

The soldier came closer and bent down a bit. "So, little girl... why are you out here all by yourself, cutting branches? And what do you have in that bag?" He looked in at the pinecones.

"You're not planning a celebration, are you?" He smiled, but it was like a wolf. "You are old enough to know that these meaningless superstitions are forbidden. Who is your papa?"

The smell of drink surrounded him like a cloud, and Riina wished that Mama knew where she was.

The soldier stood up, and now his voice echoed in the trees. "Answer me when I talk to you! Who is your papa?"

Riina opened her mouth to answer, but nothing came out. Instead, she heard a different voice, not her own. It said, "I will take my sister home now, please."

The soldier spun around, a little unsteady. There behind him, standing straight and tall, his fists clenched inside his gloves, was Kalev. He was only a few years older than Riina, but at that moment he looked so old that Riina hardly recognized him.

"I will take my sister home now, sir," he repeated, looking up at the soldier. He didn't mean it as a challenge. After all, he was shaking inside. But the soldier's anger rose like a wave, and then it crashed.

"Oh, you will?! So now you are telling me what to do? Did your father not teach you to stay in your place?" His eyes blazed with a cold fire, and he took a step toward Kalev. Inside, Riina was screaming at Kalev to *Run! Run!* But she could not make a sound.

The soldier grabbed the barrel of his rifle with both hands and swung. He knocked Kalev to the ground as if he were made of straw. For a frozen moment, Riina was a statue, holding a holly branch. The soldier swayed, trying to regain his balance. Kalev lay in the snow.

Then, suddenly come to life, Riina dropped everything and bolted past the soldier. She knelt down next to Kalev. He didn't move. She prodded his shoulder and bent close to his ear. "Kalev, are you OK?"

Slowly, he lifted his head and nodded. There was a cut on his face, and he looked dazed. Riina pulled a handkerchief from her pocket and wiped the blood from his face. "Let's go home," she said, and helped him to his feet. After a few steps, Riina glanced over her shoulder. But it was as if the soldier didn't see them anymore. He was staring at the drops of red in the white snow.

The walk home seemed to take hours. Riina wondered if the soldier would shoot at them, but it was too scary to think about. When they walked into the house, all the activity in the kitchen suddenly stopped. Mama and the girls stared at them. Then Mama said, "Don't let those cookies burn," and she took Kalev and Riina to the bedroom. She cleaned and bandaged the cut. Riina sat on the bed next to her brother, still wearing her coat and hat. She could tell Kalev was hurt, but he didn't cry.

When she finished, Mama pulled a chair in front of them and sat down. "Now you will tell me what happened. And when your Papa gets home, you will tell him, too."

Riina looked at Kalev, and he said, "You first." So she told about her idea to gather pinecones and holly, the whole dream-like blur of what happened. But then she remembered the bag of decorations left in the woods, and Papa's pocketknife, too. And she started to cry. Mama lifted Riina onto her lap and held her close.

Then Kalev told how he was pretending to track a bear by following Riina's footprints from the house into the woods. And then there were very big footprints that came along next to hers. "When I saw the soldier, I wanted to be brave... but I was afraid," he said sadly.

"Brave is what you *do*, not how you feel," Mama said. She looked up at the ceiling and sighed. "Enough for now. You will talk to Papa later." They went back to the kitchen, but even the warm smell of cookies could not dispel the cloud that had settled over the house.

When Papa came home that afternoon, he and Mama talked quietly for a minute. Then he took Kalev and Riina into the bedroom and sat down. He looked at the bandage on Kalev's face. "Mama says I need to talk to you. Do you know why?"

They both nodded, and told him the whole story. He was quiet when they finished, giving his heart time to melt the anger and fear he would not pass along to his children. Then he put his arms around them. "You didn't do anything wrong, either of you. But you were in danger with that soldier, do you understand?"

"Yes, Papa," Kalev said. But he was thinking, trying to figure something out. After a minute, he said, "Papa, why would that soldier want to hurt a boy or a girl? He's so much stronger, it's not right. You always tell me to be gentle when I play with the kids who are smaller."

Papa took a deep breath. "Things are not always as they should be. Such a man did not become cold in one day. He has been storing up darkness in his heart for a long time. Not everything that happens is good, Kalev. But good can come in the end, if we open the door."

He turned to Riina. "So your bag of decorations is left in the woods. I will go look for it before dark. Now go and see what you can do to help Mama, both of you."

Papa soon came back with the bag... but no pocketknife. "Don't be sad, little one," he said to Riina. Then, he winked. "Mama always tells me I have too many pocketknives."

That evening, the whole family cleaned every corner of the house in preparation for Christmas. Papa brought in fresh straw from the barn, and they scattered it on the floor as a reminder that the Christ child spent his first night on earth in a stable.

Maarja set an extra place at the table, for the memory of relatives who had gone before.

After dinner, everyone gathered around the fire. As usual, Papa and Kalev were carving more pieces for the nativity scene, and little curls of wood collected on the floor all around them. New sheep and oxen and shepherds appeared every Christmas, and this year there was even a new angel with wings outstretched, holding a star in both hands.

And they sang, all the songs that their people had been singing for as long as anyone could remember. The candles chased away the darkness, and the music's echo lingered in the room like voices from the past. Papa closed his eyes. "I dream of a day that we will sing these songs in a church, together with relatives and neighbors... imagine that sound! That would be like heaven to me."

The fire died down, and it was time for bed. Riina watched Mama check Kalev's bandage, but in her mind, she saw her brother standing in front of the soldier like a shield. She hugged him and went upstairs. Riina fell asleep trying to imagine hundreds of people singing Christmas songs, all together, in a church. She had never heard such a thing.

The next morning, even before she opened her eyes, Riina smelled the Christmas bread. She remembered what day it was and ran downstairs. The fire roared, breakfast sizzled, Maarja and Triinu chattered and laughed, and whiffs of pine floated throughout the house. They sat down to breakfast, joined hands, and everyone was quiet for a moment as Papa said grace.

The once-a-year treats were savored, and tea was poured many times over. No one was in a hurry to finish. Mama and Papa told stories that brought long-ago relatives to life. "You should know them even though you never met," Mama said. "They are your people." Riina felt sure that she would recognize each one if they came and sat at the empty place.

After breakfast, Papa went to the window and pulled back the shade to look outside. "Kalev!" he called, "get your boots and come outside with me. There's someone lying in the snow out there!"

Kalev scrambled for his boots and followed Papa out the door. Mama and the girls watched from the window as they dug the snow away from the body. It was a man, lying face down. Papa grabbed his arm and rolled him over, then knelt and brushed the snow away from his face. He looked for breath in the cold air, and felt the wrist for a pulse. Riina looked at Kalev's face. And then she knew. It was the soldier.

Papa lifted him up by the shoulders and motioned for Kalev to lift his feet. Mama ran to hold the door as they carried him into the house. Riina stared out the window at the empty bottle in the snow.

"Put a chair next to the fire," Papa ordered. "And get some blankets." They propped the soldier up in the chair, and Papa pulled off his boots and frozen coat.

"Is he alive?" Mama asked.

"I think so," Papa said. "But his flame is almost out. If he lives, it won't be our doing."

Papa went to hang his coat on the hook and put his boots by the door, rubbing his hands together on the way back to the fireplace. Then he noticed Riina crouching behind the table. He looked at her, puzzled. But when he saw the look on Kalev's face, the light dawned.

"So," he said. He steered Kalev by the shoulders to where Riina was hiding. He bent down next to them, and asked softly, "This man is your soldier?"

They nodded.

Papa stared at the soldier. His right hand clenched into a fist, then relaxed as he exhaled slowly. He shook his head and turned back to them.

"Kalev. Do you remember what you asked me yesterday?"

Kalev thought for a minute. "Yes, Papa."

"Yesterday this soldier was the strong one. You can see it is different today." He gently squeezed his son's arm. "Who is strong today?"

Kalev looked into his father's face. "We are."

"You are right. So do we use our strength to hurt this man? Or to help him?"

"We help him," Kalev said. It was the same voice that Riina heard in the woods the day before.

"Don't be afraid," Papa whispered.

Mama was heating broth and tea at the stove. Papa walked back to the soldier. His thawing clothes were steaming and dripping, but his face and hands were still the wrong color. Papa felt again for his pulse. "I don't know," he said. "It doesn't seem to be getting stronger."

He watched the soldier for so long that Riina thought maybe their Christmas had come to an early end. She tugged on Papa's sleeve. "We always sing," she said.

He looked down and smiled. "Of course we will sing!" Papa replied. "It's Christmas, after all. And maybe that will warm him from the inside."

They all gathered on blankets in front of the fireplace and made room for Maarja with her guitar. For a long time, they sang. Between songs, Papa read the story of the Christ child's birth and they took turns telling folk tales. The silent figure slumped in a chair was almost forgotten. But suddenly, the soldier stirred. And shivered. And groaned. And opened his eyes.

He looked around the room, trying to find out if he was dead or alive. He looked at the decorations, the nativity scene, the fireplace, the blankets. He tried to speak, but nothing came out. Then he tried again and said, in a hoarse voice, "The singing. I thought it was angels."

Maarja started another song. The soldier closed his eyes.

Mama went to the kitchen and came back with a bowl of broth and a mug of tea. "We found you in the snow," Papa said. The soldier cautiously sipped the steaming broth. He looked slowly from face to face, and Riina wondered if he would recognize her. When their eyes met, he froze. Then he looked over at Kalev. He saw the bandage, and it all came rushing back. His shoulders drooped, and he stared into the bowl.

Maarja and Triinu went to the kitchen with Mama to set out food for the Christmas meal. Riina and Kalev huddled around the nativity scene, examining the figures and looking for new ones that had appeared overnight. The soldier stood up, unsteady. "I don't belong here," he said softly, as if to himself, and fumbled with his boots.

"But you are our guest today," Papa replied. "It is our honor to share this meal with you. You are welcome to stay."

The soldier hesitated. He looked at the table, nodded once to Papa, and sat down again. But he couldn't bring himself to look at Riina or Kalev.

When the time came to gather around the table, Papa guided the soldier to the empty place. *Praise God from Whom all blessings flow...* Mama's clear voice was joined by the others. The *Amen* died away, blessing the feast to body and soul. And it was a feast, from beginning to end. Finally, when no one could eat another bite, the soldier cleared his throat and pushed his chair back from the table. He stood up, but his eyes were fixed on the floor. "I... I never had a meal like this in my life." The words came out as if he were trying to speak a different language. "I don't deserve it. Thank you. I must go."

He stumbled to the door under the weight of an invisible burden. Papa followed and helped him with his coat. The soldier slumped heavily against the door. Then he said to Papa, almost in a whisper, "I must speak to your son and daughter."

"Kalev. Riina. Come here."

Kalev took Riina's hand and they walked slowly over to Papa. The soldier bent down on one knee and looked into their eyes. "Little girl," he said to Riina, "I'm sorry." Somehow he didn't look like the soldier in the woods any more. She nodded.

He turned to Kalev. "Young man," he said, "you are very

brave, and I'm sorry I hurt you." Kalev stood at attention, very serious. Then he reached out and shook the soldier's hand.

The soldier took a deep breath and stood up. Papa put a hand on his shoulder and said, "The light has come today. Go in peace."

The soldier opened the door. He paused, reached into his coat pocket, and handed something to Papa. With one more look at Riina and Kalev, he walked out into the snow. Papa watched him go. He closed the door. He hugged his children. Then he opened his hand so they could see. It was his pocketknife.

AMOS

A chorus of stars and a thin crescent moon sent a shadowy light across the barren landscape. It was barely enough to keep the dark fingers of night at bay.

Micah picked his way across the rocky ground, his eyes fixed on the glow of a distant fire. He could feel the heartbeat of the little lamb he held close to his chest. "Don't worry now, we're almost back with the others," he said softly.

Before long, he was close enough to see silhouettes of the other shepherds by the fire. As he entered the circle of light, they looked up. "So you found her, eh? Took you long enough. We thought maybe you'd be spending the night with the jackals." Micah walked through their laughter and headed straight for old Amos. He sat down.

"So she give you some trouble, did she?" Amos asked with a smile.

"A little," Micah said. "It took a long time to find her. Then when I did, she was in the thorns and didn't want to come out. I had to crawl in after her."

"Got you a little scratched up too, I see." Amos took the lamb and checked her gently. "She's not hurt, just scared. Go put her with the others, that's what she needs."

Micah took the lamb and walked slowly to the pen. He would have liked to sit by the fire and hold her a while longer but, being the youngest of the group, he didn't need to give the others one more reason to tease him. He put the lamb next to some of the ewes, and she snuggled happily.

Micah lingered to gaze up at the sparkling expanse of sky. Concentration lined his face as he listened intently. There was only the muffled sound of the sheep, and a distant howl. The chill of the night air soon brought him back to the fire. He poked the embers and coaxed a bit of flame to life, then wrapped himself in a blanket and settled down next to Amos.

Most of the other shepherds were asleep. Micah watched the fire for a while and thought of his struggle to find the lost lamb. A jackal howled again, closer now, and Micah shivered.

"Amos?" he whispered.

"Mmm hmm..."

"Tell me again about the night of the angels."

For a moment, except for the crackle of the fire, everything was perfectly still. Then Amos drew a deep breath. He rolled over and looked at Micah, but his eyes were far away.

"There was nothing special about that night. We gathered up the sheep, ate our food, sat around the fire. It was cold and clear... just the same as any other night."

Amos looked up at the sky, then closed his eyes. He could see it all, just as it had happened. He had seen it every night since then, whenever he closed his eyes.

"Then, just like that, there he was. An angel, more magnificent than anything you can imagine, right there in front of us. The light... it's as if he was *made* of light, coming from the inside... and not just *light*, but... the glory of God Himself blazing like a fire all around us.

"I thought right then I would die. We all did. It didn't seem possible to see such a thing and live. But the angel said, *Do not be afraid!* His voice was like rolling thunder."

Amos chuckled. "I was still afraid, I couldn't help myself. But it didn't stop me from hearing every word.

"He said, *Listen, I bring you glorious news of great joy which is for all the people. This very day, in David's town, a Savior has been born for you. He is Christ, the Lord. Let this prove it to you: you will find a baby, wrapped up and lying in a manger.*

"And then..." Amos's voice faltered. "We didn't see them come, just all of a sudden there they were. As many as the stars! The armies of Heaven, praising God. *Glory to God in the highest Heaven! Peace on earth among men of goodwill!*" He shook his head. "You never heard such a sound."

Amos was silent for a long time. Micah was afraid he wouldn't tell the rest of the story. But eventually he continued. "Then they left us. They went back to Heaven. We didn't waste any time, we ran as fast as we could, all the way to Bethlehem. And before long, we found the tiny baby boy lying in a manger in one of the stables. We told his father and mother — Joseph and Mary — everything that we had heard and seen, and what the angel said about the baby. We told everyone! They could hardly believe it." Amos paused, remembering. "His mother, though... she took it all in, like it was a secret treasure in her heart.

"We went back to our work. But we couldn't stop praising God, because we found everything just as the angel said it would be."

Amos looked at Micah and smiled. "You never tire of hearing it, do you?" he asked.

Micah shook his head. "Never." But there was a question in his mind that he had never asked.

"Amos," he said. "What happened to that baby?"

Amos's face clouded a bit. "I don't know, Micah. I've asked myself that same question many times, all these years. The world is a dangerous place, especially... especially for a tiny baby..." His voice trailed off and then found its way again. "But if all Heaven took notice of that little one, the way it happened that night... well, it may be that great joy is still to come. I just hope I live to see it."

Amos reached over and tucked Micah's blanket around him. "Now go to sleep."

⊰——⊱

The years passed, and Micah grew tall and strong. He still worked as a shepherd, but now he had a flock of his own. And by now Amos was a very old man, no longer able to work in the fields. But Micah did not forget his friend, and often stopped to visit him or ask his advice about the sheep. Amos would still tell about the angels when asked, but Micah noticed that he sometimes seemed troubled after telling the story.

One day Micah set out for a nearby village to look at some sheep for his flock. As he walked along the road, he wished Amos was strong enough to join him. He had the best eye when it came to choosing animals.

Micah reached the top of a small ridge and looked down into the valley below. He stopped. It was filled with people, more than the combined population of all the villages for miles around. Puzzled, he wondered what — besides trouble — could bring so many people together. He considered another path to avoid the crowd. But his curiosity was stronger.

As he got closer, Micah elbowed his way toward what seemed to be the center. He saw a man sitting on the side of the hill, talking to the people. *Just another traveling rabbi. But why such a crowd?* He inched close enough to hear, and then he noticed a small child sitting next to the teacher.

The words came clearly. "Believe me, unless you change your whole outlook and become like little children you will never enter the kingdom of Heaven. It is the man who can be as humble as this little child who is greatest in the kingdom of Heaven. Be careful that you never despise a single one of these little ones — for I tell you that they have angels who see my Father's face continuously in Heaven."

Angels! Micah thought of Amos. But he pushed the thought away and just listened.

"What do you think? If a man has a hundred sheep and one wanders away from the rest, won't he leave the ninety-nine on the hillside and set out to look for the one who has wandered away?"

"Of course he will," Micah murmured.

The teacher continued, "Yes, and if he should chance to find it I assure you he is more delighted over that one than he is over the ninety-nine who never wandered away."

Micah smiled, and nodded.

"You can understand then that it is never the will of your Father in Heaven that a single one of these little ones should be lost."

The teacher continued on, telling stories. Micah forgot about his errand, captured by the teacher's words. He had never heard anything like this. But then something happened that took his breath away.

A man pushed past Micah, carrying a young girl. Her arms were clasped tightly around his neck, but her legs hung limp and useless. Micah watched as the man made his way to the teacher, laid the girl down gently in front of him, and knelt beside her. Micah could not hear the man's words, but he was obviously pleading with the teacher for some reason. Rather than being annoyed by this interruption, Micah watched as the teacher's face flooded with compassion. He put his hand on the man's shoulder and knelt next to him, speaking softly to the little girl. Then he took the girl's hand in both of his own, stood up, and helped her slowly to her feet. She stood uncertainly for a moment, like a newborn lamb, then took a few steps. A smile dawned on her face, then with a squeal of delight she ran into the teacher's open arms. Together, they helped the man to his feet. Tears were streaming down his face. Micah heard the teacher say, "It is your faith that has healed your daughter... go home in peace." Hand in hand, father and daughter made their way along the narrow path that opened through the crowd.

Micah couldn't believe his eyes. He felt weak and off-balance. Now it was as if the floodgates had opened, and a steady stream of shipwrecked humanity flowed to the teacher. With a touch he healed each one, sending a ripple of joy back through the crowd.

It was then, as he watched, that Micah felt a familiar stirring in his heart. Like a longing and a coming home, it echoed inside him whenever he heard Amos tell of the night of angels. *But why now? Unless...*

Micah turned abruptly to an old man next to him.

"Sir!" he blurted. "The teacher... who is he?"

Startled, the man replied, "You mean his name? It's Jesus."

"Where is he from?"

"Nazareth, in Galilee."

"He was born there?"

"Well, I would assume so." The man smiled. "Most people are born where they're from. But if you really want to know, you can ask his mother." He scanned the crowd near the teacher, then pointed. "She's over there, in that group of women. With the blue shawl. See?"

Micah looked and nodded. His heart pounded, and he could barely speak.

"Do you know her name?"

Micah heard the reply, though it sounded like it came through a long tunnel.

"Yes. His mother's name is Mary."

Micah made his way slowly toward the group of women, as if he were crossing a narrow bridge. The noise of the crowd faded away, and he remembered the angel's words to Amos: *Do not be afraid.* He hesitated on the edge of the group, waiting. Finally, the teacher's mother turned in his direction.

Micah came near with a few tentative steps and found his voice. "Ma'am, my name is Micah. I'm a shepherd outside Bethlehem. I... I have a friend, Amos. He was a shepherd, too, but now he is old and frail. All these years, he's... he's told me about..." Micah paused and caught a breath of courage. "About the night of the angels. And a baby boy... in a manger... and the baby's parents, Joseph and Mary." The lump in his throat stopped him for a moment. "It's heavy on his heart...what became of the baby."

As Micah watched, he saw the answer in Mary's eyes. Through tears, she said softly, "Tell your friend you have found the baby. May he have peace."

Micah bowed in gratitude, his hands on his heart. He moved away from the women and was drawn into the circle of people surrounding Jesus. He heard some men saying, "We were sent to ask, are you the one who is to come, or are we to look for someone else?"

Then Micah heard Jesus reply. It was the treasure of great joy, which he would carry back to Amos.

> Go and tell what you have seen and heard. The blind are recovering their sight, cripples are walking again, lepers being healed, the deaf hearing, dead men are being brought to life again, and the good news is being given to those in need. And happy is the man who never loses his faith in me.

CAMERA

After Thanksgiving, everything snowballs to Christmas. Like riding a sled down an icy slope, I sometimes hang on and squint as the moments go skidding by, unable to steer or stop, hoping all along there is no tree in my path at the bottom. The minutes of each day shrink like a wool sweater in a hot dryer, coming out only big enough for a Chihuahua.

But at other times, moments flow like a walk through a snowy wood, and the pleasures of the season can be savored... lights and decorations, baking (and eating) Christmas cookies, Alastair Sim as Scrooge, the yearly appearance of oyster pudding, handsome nutcrackers, *A Child's Christmas in Wales*.

As I gathered Christmas decorations from various closets, I was caught somewhere between the pell-mell sled ride and the snowy walk. From the stereo, Miss Piggy belted out "F-i-v-e G-o-o-o-l-d R-i-n-g-s" in the Muppets' rendition of The Twelve Days of Christmas. I smiled, then frowned into the closet as I realized the nutcracker boxes were blocked in behind another box of—*what?* Soon I was sitting on the floor sifting through old family photos. The silent eye that captured all those moments gazed at me from its place on the bookshelf, great-uncle Willie's five-pound 1947 Graflex camera.

It was as if I looked over Willie's shoulder as he took all the pictures, hearing the laughter that paused just long enough for the POP! of the big blue flash bulb. Pop-pop pulling Grammy on a sled, Nanny reading her Bible by the light of a lamp, Uncle Clyde's big smile and gentle eyes, little me watching wide-eyed as Pop-pop tends a very big turkey, Dad and his grandpop with their shotguns, showing off two pheasants and three rabbits. People I belong to, who — as Grammy would say — "aren't here no more." I put the photos back into the box, but their pulse was still beating.

⚜ — ⚜

The seasonal flurry of cards, concerts, and festivities came to rest on Christmas Eve. I spent the evening baking cranberry-orange bread and reading *The Story of the Other Wise Man*. The little loaves came out of the oven just in time. I grabbed coat and gloves, threw them into the car, and drove off to the midnight service in Quakertown.

The Pleiades and Auriga glittered overhead. Orion rose in the southeast, and Cassiopeia hovered in the northwest. Time suspended, like the stars, watching, waiting.

The candlelit church glowed, and its warmth reached into the night as I opened the door. Down a long hallway, distant voices sang Adeste Fideles, as the choir slowly approached. When they reached the sanctuary, the organ and all the faithful joined in…

> *Yea, Lord we greet Thee, Born this happy morning,*
> *Jesus, to Thee be all glory given;*
> *Word of the Father, Now in flesh appearing:*
> *O come, let us adore Him, O come, let us adore Him,*
> *O come, let us adore Him, Christ the Lord.*

The music and message became a prism, focusing all the lights of the season on a stable in Bethlehem, the awe-inspiring mystery of Emmanuel — "God with us."

> *Because the heart of our God is full of mercy towards us,*
> *the first light of Heaven shall come to visit us — to shine on*
> *those who lie in darkness and under the shadow of death,*
> *and to guide our feet in the path of peace.*

The echo of Isaiah's words breathed life into one tiny flame, passed from candle to candle, hand to hand, a hundred little messengers of light. *The light shines in the darkness, and the darkness has not overcome it.* The bells of Christmas rang out a joyful benediction and followed me outside into the midnight.

I walked out Fourth Street to Juniper and stood in front of 402 for a long time. When I left that house for the last time, I gathered up all the memories and brought them with me. So now I can see, clearly, my parents and me climbing the front porch steps, shopping bags full of gifts. We ring the bell and walk in, and Grammy meets us in the narrow hallway, wearing a Christmas apron. "Take off your things!" Willie and Clyde's gifts are stacked on the steps that lead upstairs. We put our coats on the bed and I walk back to the kitchen to hug Pop-pop and say Merry Christmas.

The scene got blurry. I wiped tears away with the back of my glove and continued up Juniper Street to Main. My memories of Nanny's house are contained in that box of snapshots in my closet, along with stories that happened before I was born. Standing there on the sidewalk, it wasn't hard to believe that if I went up to the front window and looked in, I would see all those people in the photos.

Snowflakes meandered through the glow of streetlights. I turned away and walked slowly back down Juniper Street. Seeping into the quiet came the sound of carolers...

> *Christians, awake! salute the happy morn*
> *Whereon the Savior of the world was born;*
> *Rise to adore the mystery of love,*
> *Which hosts of angels chanted from above;*
> *With them the joyful tidings first begun*
> *Of God Incarnate and the virgin's Son.*

I stopped to listen. It was hard to tell which direction it was coming from. I couldn't see anyone. The music followed me as I walked back to my car, but the carolers remained out of sight.

I cranked up the heat and stopped at Wawa to get a cup of hot chocolate for the ride home.

⇥——⇤

That night, I woke from a sound sleep. Opened my eyes and looked at the clock. 4:23. Listened. The house was quiet. Not even the faint hum of the heater. Then I heard it. Voices. Faint at first, then stronger. Singing.

I got up and went to the front door, moved the shade aside with one finger, and peeked out.

They were in the front yard, just beyond the porch, silhouetted against dim lights across the street. The sound of voices singing in the cold air of Christmas Eve can take your breath away. And there was a warmth woven into these notes, a familiarity somewhere between déjà vu and a dream, that made my heart beat faster.

> *Then may we hope, th'angelic hosts among,*
> *To sing, redeemed, a glad triumphal song;*
> *He that was born upon this joyful day*
> *Around us all His glory shall display;*
> *Saved by His love, forever we shall sing*
> *Eternal praise to heaven's almighty King.*

My camera was on the table. I picked it up, opened the door, and took a picture. For a split second, the flash lit the mysterious carolers — and the smiling faces were those I had seen in the old photos.

I blinked, and the night was silent once again.

CROSSING

The horizon glowed with a promise of the sun as Mordecai trudged along the dusty path. A bag of spices hung heavily on his shoulder, and he steadied himself with his staff. He had left many footprints on this road and knew its dangers, though now his eyes were not as sharp to spot them. Mordecai's nephew sometimes made the trip to market with him, and he always felt safer with that strong boy at his side. But today he was alone, and softly repeated the scriptures to quiet his heart.

> *Arise, shine, for your light has come, and the glory of the Lord rises upon you. See, darkness covers the earth and thick darkness is over the people, but the Lord rises upon you and his glory appears over you. Nations will come to your light, and kings to the brightness of your dawn.*

Mordecai's voice trailed off and his heart skipped a beat. There was movement on the path ahead. Unthinking, his hand tightened its grip on the staff, his back straightened and shoulders squared, and his legs took each step with purpose. He gazed straight at the approaching figures, though at this distance, they were shapeless lumps.

As his eyes focused, Mordecai's fear turned to curiosity. He saw a man leading a donkey, gripping the harness with a strong hand. A young woman was riding on the donkey and cradling a very small child in her arms. She did not look up. Mordecai spoke a greeting to the stranger, who only nodded in reply. The wear and tear of a long journey was written on the man's face, and a burden much heavier than the small bundle on his back.

Mordecai continued on to the town and joined the bustle of the market. He spent the day haggling with customers over prices and commiserating with fellow merchants over taxes. The couple didn't enter his mind again until he was on the road back to his village. "Too dangerous!" Mordecai muttered, shaking his head. "On the road at that hour with a woman and baby. These young people, they have no sense."

The next morning, Mordecai climbed a ladder to survey his roof, checking the damage from a recent storm. There were broken tiles, and he also discovered beams in need of repair. This would have been an easy project when he was younger.

"I could help you with that."

Startled, Mordecai looked down. It was the stranger he had passed on the road. A light of recognition flickered across each man's face.

"You could, eh?" Mordecai slowly climbed down. "I saw you on the road yesterday. You're not from around here."

The man hesitated. "Well, I guess you could say I am now. We're renting a place from Jacob on the other side of the village." Indecision clouded his face, then he added, "My name is Joseph, and we came here from Judea. That was my wife and son with me yesterday."

Mordecai's bushy eyebrows shot up. "Judea! Long way from there to this little village in Egypt." He paused for an explanation, but none came.

Instead, Joseph shifted from one foot to the other. "I'm a carpenter," he said. "I can help with your roof."

Mordecai studied the young man, then smiled. "Well, Joseph, there are plenty of things falling apart in this village, so you should have no trouble finding work. And you might as well start with my roof."

Joseph's face softened, and he took Mordecai's hand. "Thank you. I'll get my tools and come back right away."

Mordecai wasn't one to stand by and watch someone else work, so he helped where he could and left the heavy labor to Joseph. They worked side by side all morning, but only a handful of words passed between them. Mordecai quickly saw that he had not made a mistake in hiring this stranger. Joseph was sure of himself and worked carefully. He seemed completely absorbed in the work — or else his mind was miles away. Mordecai didn't know which.

As the days and weeks rolled by, Mordecai met Joseph often in the village. He always stopped to talk, and after a time Mordecai was pleased to see the hint of a smile on Joseph's face when they met. Whenever Mordecai needed help with anything, Joseph was usually there without being asked, and he soon refused to take any money. So Mordecai resorted to bringing cheese or vegetables from the market to Joseph's door as payment. He became a frequent guest at their table, and the warmth of being included in this little family brought joy to his heart. He especially loved when Joseph's young son crawled over to him to be picked up. The boy laughed and buried his face in Mordecai's shoulder. At those moments, Mordecai's aches and pains — and the grumpiness that sometimes came with them — melted away.

But for all the light of those times, Mordecai also sensed a shadow. It crept across his mind at night when he couldn't sleep. He had known Joseph for many months, and they talked quite often and at length. But no mention was made of his family's life in Judea or why they had come on this long journey to Egypt. It was obvious they had no family here. Mordecai had made subtle attempts to steer the conversation in that direction, but Joseph never once gave even a tidbit of information. But what really stuck in Mordecai's mind were the times when he caught a glimpse of Joseph's face as he watched his son at play. It spoke of fear and tenderness and determination and helplessness, and Mordecai could not imagine the story it told. His friend carried a great secret, but whether it was a diamond or a dagger, Mordecai could not tell.

One night as Mordecai lay awake, he thought of all the times Joseph had helped him — beginning with the first day they arrived in the village. *My young friend has carried many loads for me. I am not strong like he is, but maybe I can help him carry this burden in his heart... if he will let me.*

The next morning, Mordecai circled the village in search of Joseph. He found him on the road with his donkey and a cart loaded with wood. Mordecai walked with him, but barely spoke a word. Before long, Joseph said with a smile, "You lost your voice in the night?"

Mordecai chuckled. He reached out and rubbed the donkey's neck as he searched for words. "Joseph," he began, "I have known you for many months now. You have become like a relative to me, and I hope I do not offend you with what I am going to say. But I am an old man, and we worry less about offending and more about what is on our minds."

Joseph stopped the donkey and turned to Mordecai as he continued. "I watch you, Joseph. I watch you while you look at your son. I don't know who you are or where you come from, but on your face I see the thoughts you will not speak. They are in a language I do not know, but they are heavy for you."

Joseph stared off into the distance and exhaled deeply, as if he had been holding his breath. He turned back to Mordecai and said, "You complain about your eyesight, Mordecai. But you see clearly with the eyes of the heart. The time is right. Tonight, after my son is asleep, I will come to your house."

❧ — ❧

The first stars were just beginning to twinkle in the dark blue sky as Mordecai came out of his house. A faint glow hung on the western horizon where the sun had slipped into its resting place. He sat on a bench and looked up. Each of the stars had its place, night after night. Most nights he came outside to watch them before he went to sleep. A light breeze rustled in the trees, and soon he heard footsteps. Joseph joined him on the bench and sat in silence for a few minutes, looking at the sky.

"You might think I'm crazy when I tell you," Joseph began. "Or a liar."

Mordecai smiled. "You don't strike me as either."

"I'm not," Joseph said. "But don't change your mind." He took a deep breath.

"It all started when I was engaged to Mary. I found out… it became known that she was pregnant. And not by me."

Mordecai stiffened, but said nothing. This was not the beginning he expected.

"The whole world turned upside down, and I didn't know what to do. It was awful. I couldn't think, and I felt sick. But I still cared about her and didn't want her to be disgraced, so I thought maybe the best way was to break off the engagement, but do it quietly. You know how people talk."

Joseph paused. "My mind was still unsettled. I couldn't decide. And then… I'm telling you the truth… an angel of the Lord came to me in a dream. He called me by name! He said, *Joseph, do not be afraid to take Mary as your wife! What she has conceived is conceived through the Holy Spirit, and she will give birth to a son, whom you will call Jesus, for it is he who will save his people from their sins.*"

Mordecai felt a little faint and was glad to be sitting down. *An angel!? When do angels speak to carpenters? And when does a woman become pregnant without a man?* But Joseph was already continuing.

"We had to go to Bethlehem for the census, and it was not an easy journey. Mary was about to deliver, and we couldn't find a room anywhere in the town. So we ended up in a stable, and that night the baby was born."

"Oh, no," Mordecai groaned. "In a stable?!"

Joseph smiled ruefully. "It turned out to be all right. Mary wrapped the baby up and put him in the manger for a cradle. I think having the animals nearby helped him sleep."

"What about Mary?" Mordecai asked.

The moon was climbing from the eastern horizon, and by its light Mordecai saw tears filling Joseph's eyes. For a few minutes he couldn't answer.

"What I didn't tell you is that an angel also came to Mary, while we were engaged. He called her by name, too, and told her that she would conceive a son by the power of the Holy Spirit, and he would be great and be known as the Son of the Most High.

"Her response to the angel was *I belong to the Lord, body and soul. Let it happen as you say.* She lives in God's world, Mordecai. No matter what happens." Joseph blinked, and then brushed away the tears.

"But I didn't finish telling you about the night in the stable. Everything had settled down a little bit. It was quiet, and the baby was asleep. All of a sudden I heard footsteps outside, and into the stable comes a shepherd. He looks around at us, then calls out the door — *Here, they're in here!* More shepherds come in, and they gather around the baby, just looking at him as if he dropped down from the sky.

"I couldn't understand why they were there, and they all started whispering at once, but finally it came out that they had been in the fields with the sheep, when an angel stood before them, blazing with glory. He told them that a Savior had been born that night in Bethlehem, and the proof would be that they would find a baby wrapped up and lying in a manger. Then they said the one angel was joined by more than they could count, praising God."

Mordecai stared at Joseph, stunned. He couldn't comprehend or even imagine most of what Joseph had said. He closed his eyes and rubbed his forehead. It was all swirling in his head like a dream, and he tried to make himself wake up.

Joseph put his hand on Mordecai's shoulder. "Mordecai, are

you all right?" he asked gently. "There's more to tell... should I go on?" Mordecai nodded.

"We stayed in Bethlehem after the baby was born. One day we had a strange visit. A caravan of magi from the east came to the door. They said they had come to honor the child born to be king of the Jews. When they saw the baby they knelt down and gave him gifts — gold, frankincense, myrrh. And do you know how they found us?"

Mordecai shook his head, but then said, "Angels?"

"No. They said a star guided them to the place we were staying. A star. All the way from the east to a little house in Bethlehem. Well, they had stopped in Jerusalem first, asking about the child. Which explains what happened next.

"After they left, an angel appeared to me in a dream and said, *Get up now, take the little child and his mother and escape to Egypt. Stay there until I tell you. For Herod means to seek out the child and kill him!* We left that same night, and for the whole journey I imagined soldiers with swords around every corner. But what could I do against Herod's soldiers?" In Joseph's desperate eyes, Mordecai finally recognized the terrible treasure.

"Joseph," Mordecai said, "I know you would protect the boy with your very life. But from what you have told me, heaven itself holds him in its hand."

Joseph nodded. "It is true, and a good thing. I have never felt so small as I feel now, telling you all this. It's bigger than the sky with all its stars." He looked up into the night and sighed. "Mordecai, there is only one thing more, and now I see this is the hardest of all. Two nights ago, an angel appeared to me again in a dream and said that we are to return to Israel. Those who intended to kill the child are dead. We will leave the day after tomorrow."

Joseph's words lingered in the air. Mordecai felt his world stand still. Joseph took Mordecai's hand in both of his. "You have become an uncle to me and my family. It is God who made our paths cross, and he will guide our steps in the days to come."

Mordecai smiled and nodded. "And I am thankful for the crossing."

"Come to supper tomorrow night," Joseph said.

"I will be early," Mordecai replied.

That night, Mordecai's dreams were filled with angels and kings, shepherds and swords. He woke up exhausted and dazed. All day, images and phrases from Joseph's story threaded themselves into a tangle that he could not unravel. The sun crawled across the sky, until at last it was time to walk down the road to Joseph's house.

From a distance, he could see Joseph outside with his son, waiting. He smiled as Mordecai approached and, without a word, lifted the boy into his arms. Mordecai held the child close to his chest. Little arms circled his neck, and he felt the heartbeat of heaven.

⊷ — ⊶

The next morning, Mordecai opened his eyes before dawn and went outside to watch the sun rise. He noticed a tiny cloth bag tacked to his door. Carefully, he opened it, and its treasures fell into his hand. Gold, frankincense, and myrrh.

DREAM

The after-work traffic was thick as eggnog and spiked with mid-December urgency. A silver Cooper sporting Rudolph antlers and a red nose darted across three lanes of traffic and cut me off. It swerved into Starbucks, and I tried to keep my inner Grinch at bay.

I had one eye on the dashboard clock. It blinked the passing minutes while I waited for lights to change. As I pulled into the nursing home entrance with a little too much zip for the speed bump, the accumulated agitation finally bounced away. I was almost on time. A whiff of captive air escaped through the double glass doors before they closed behind me. Wheelchair traffic was heavy in the narrow hallway, and it was a challenge to reach the room where my fellow choir members were assembled. They were a forest of green, black, and red, decked with festive pins, Christmas ties, and the occasional flashing bulb. I merged in with the altos, and in a few minutes the line lurched forward, propelled by good humor.

From the auditorium's small stage, we looked out at row upon row of wheelchairs and walkers. In spite of appearances, I knew that the spark of life burned bright behind those faces. The feeble organ and piano gave out the first notes of O Come All Ye Faithful, and we sang with all our hearts. In fact, our hearts sometimes got the better of our voices and, instead of words, only tears could squeeze out. But no matter. Song by song, all of us together became a choir of the bent and broken, joining our hearts with the music of heaven.

At 8:00 sharp, the program ended and the slow, rolling exodus began amid smiles and wishes of Merry Christmas. I greeted as many residents as possible, startled — as always — by small, frail women with vice-grip handshakes.

In passing, I took the hand of a man slumped in a wheelchair. "Merry Christmas!"

He looked up. "Merry Christmas. You sing good."

I smiled. "Thanks. We all enjoy coming here every year."

He still had my hand and now the aide was pushing him along, so I walked beside, bending over a bit so I could hear him.

"Like angels." He looked as if there was something else on his mind, then it came to him. "Like stars. I had a dream," he said. "I want to tell it to you."

I glanced at the aide, but she was committed to the schedule and hadn't heard.

"Well, it looks like it's time for you to go to your room right now..." I trailed off, and just then the aide broke in.

"Come on now, Mr. Stan, let go her hand, we gotta get you back and ready for bed."

His grip did not loosen. Hoping to avert trouble, I said the first helpful thing that came to mind. "How about if I come back another time and you can tell me then?"

There was a long moment. A spark of hope kindled in his eyes, and was quickly extinguished by shadows of other promised visits. He looked down, nodded, and let go of my hand.

I stood still in the middle of the hallway as they wheeled around the corner. Then a voice in the back of my mind launched into a spirited monologue as I headed for the refreshment room... "What were you thinking?! You just promised to visit that man! When are you going to have time to do that? And drive all the way up here again. And what *dream*, anyway?

He'll forget it by the time you come back." It continued with more of the same.

I sipped punch and nibbled a few cookies, then muttered my reply. "Enough. Just stop." I took some pretzels for the road and walked outside to the car.

The earlier traffic had evaporated, and I followed the winding road out of the city. The glow of electricity faded quickly, replaced by the rising half moon and a sprinkling of stars. Small farms nestled against the hillside, and one-traffic-light towns poked holes in the darkness. It was a silent night, but the heavenly peace was disturbed by that skeptic in my head.

—⧓——⧓—

A few days later, the morning sun streamed into the kitchen. Rising through the rays, steam from my coffee revealed every air current, swirling just like my thoughts. My promised visit felt like luggage without wheels, heavy and in the way. But then, through a pinhole of grace, I saw myself in a wheelchair. The swirling stopped. I poured coffee in a to-go cup and grabbed my keys.

At the nursing home, the woman behind the front desk looked up as I approached.

"Hello, can I help you?"

"Yes, I'm here to visit someone."

She looked down and shuffled some papers. "Name?"

"I don't know."

She looked up again. "You're visiting someone and you don't know their name."

"That's right." I imagined the coffee break story in which I would play a leading role. "I was here with the choir one night last week. I met a gentleman on my way out and I would like to visit him, but I don't know his" — and suddenly the aide's voice echoed in my mind — "Stan! His name is Stan. But I don't know his room number."

She checked a list. "Room 232. Down this hall and take a right. But here, sign in first."

I walked slowly down the hall to 232 and knocked softly at the open door. He was looking out the window. "Mr. Stan?"

He straightened up a bit and looked in my direction. "Who are you?"

"I met you last week. I sang in the choir."

He remembered. "You came back."

"I wanted to hear about your dream."

He looked around the room and realized there was nowhere for me to sit. "We could go to the auditorium. They got Christmas lights in there, it's nice. And quiet too."

I wheeled him to the auditorium and found a folding chair for myself.

"I can't remember much these days, but that dream I can't forget." His eyes twinkled with a wry smile. "Nobody wants to hear it, though. People are too busy to listen."

I nodded, as one of them. He took a deep breath and began…

"I was in my house. You know how dreams are — it didn't look the same, but I understood it to be my house.

"It was a lot bigger, with lots of rooms. Each room had its own… well… story, you might say. I wandered from one room to the next, not sure what I would find. Some were good, like hunting and fishing with Pop and my uncles when I was a boy, or Christmas dinner at Aunt Ellen's. It wasn't like just having a memory in your mind. It was like walking into that time again, with all the sounds and smells and feelings that went with it."

He hoisted himself up a little bit, leaning his elbows on the arms of the wheelchair.

"But there was bad, too… real bad. I walked into the War and I almost froze." He shook his head and looked away. "Things you could never tell anybody," he said softly.

"After that I was more cautious. Eventually I came to courting my wife, and our children when they were little. It was hard to leave those rooms. On and on it went, like a maze. After a time

I found a chair, and it felt good to sit down. I put my feet up. It was like being at home inside the life I had built. Like a cat in front of the fireplace."

He paused, and I balanced on that picture, waiting for what came next.

"That's when I first heard it. I suspect it had been going on all along without me taking notice. A few taps, then quiet. Then a few more. But so soft you could barely make it out. If you were busy or had the TV on you would never hear it.

"I got up to look for the door and find out who was knocking. I went up and down every hallway, and before long I got uneasy, like there was a secret following me around. As soon as I stood still it caught up with me. *There is no door.*

"Somehow it felt like I lost everything. What if I had built myself a prison?" His urgent gaze reflected my own.

"But then… tap, tap, tap. Closer now, like it was right next to me. I looked around and there was a narrow opening. I didn't see it before. I had to go sideways to get through. At the end was a door."

He reached out his hand into the dream. "I turned the knob, very slow, and pushed it open. When I stepped out it was night, crystal clear, filled with stars. And then I saw it." Wonder, and a smile, crept across his face. "One star, shining like the light of the world. The rays went straight to my heart."

He nodded slowly.

"Now I understood who was knocking. There was music, like all the stars were singing. I could hear my little voice singing too."

Mr. Stan closed his eyes. We listened to the stars until an aide came looking for him at lunchtime.

SCARF

It was no use. No matter how hard he tried to run faster, David felt like he was standing still. Nellie was gaining on him. Even without looking over his shoulder, he knew it. A galloping mass of dark fur punctuated by bright eyes and a wet nose, it was only a matter of time and then — whump —"HELP!"—"WOOF!"— and down he tumbled into the snow with Nellie on top, firmly gripping his right boot in her mouth, shaking it just as if it was an old stuffed sock.

"David!" It was his father's voice, but very far away.

Why doesn't he come and help me? David wondered, trying to reclaim his foot from Nellie's grasp.

"David, time to get up," said his father's voice this time, but closer now.

In that fuzzy moment of awareness, David felt the dream sliding away. He opened his eyes. Papa stood at the end of the bed, shaking David's foot through the quilt.

"Get washed and dressed," Papa said softly. "But don't wake your brothers."

A brilliant crescent moon shone through the small, frosty window. Through the round iron grate in the floor came a wisp of warmth from the coal stove in the front room, and with it, the smell of cornmeal mush and potatoes frying on the stove.

Then, like a jack-in-the-box, David popped up. He had just remembered what day it was.

Carefully, he crawled out from under the quilt. His two older brothers were snoring softly on either side, so David crept down the center of the bed and hopped off the end. He poured water into the basin and washed quickly, then wet his hair and combed it with more vigor than design. Mama had laid out his clothes the night before, and within seconds David was dressed and running softly down the stairs in his wool socks.

He skidded across the linoleum floor and arrived at the middle of the kitchen. Papa was sitting at the table, watching steam rise from his coffee. Mama looked over her shoulder from the stove.

"Maybe you have enough energy already this morning and don't need breakfast." The twinkle in her eye told David she was just teasing, and he smiled. She brought a plate of mush and potatoes to the table, and David sat next to Papa.

"You say grace this morning," Papa said.

David folded his hands and closed his eyes. It all came out at high speed. "God is great and God is good and we thank Him for our food by His hand we all are fed give us Lord our daily bread amen."

Some people, when they are excited, lose their appetite. David was not such a one. Just like Papa, he spread molasses on the mush and shook salt and pepper onto the potatoes. They ate intently, in silence, and Mama chuckled at the resemblance.

Papa finished his coffee and pulled the watch from his vest pocket. The chain gleamed as he pushed the stem, and the cover opened. He held it so David could see.

"Five... umm... five..." Under his breath, David counted the minutes. "Eight minutes past five."

"The train comes at half past," his father said. "It's time to go. Get your coat and give your mother a kiss."

David sat on the floor and pulled on his boots. He took his coat from the peg and searched the sleeves and pockets for a scarf, hat, and mittens — all knitted by one or another of the aunties.

He stood in front of Mama for a final inspection.

"Honey, you have to remember to comb your hair in the morning," she said as she fixed it.

"But I *did* comb it!" David replied in disbelief.

"All right. Give me a kiss."

Mama's parting instructions came as David opened the back door and ran down the steps. "Stay with your father! And remember your manners!"

"Don't worry, Annie, he'll be fine," Papa said with a smile.

She turned to him, adjusted the pin on his conductor's coat and straightened his tie. "I know, Allen," she said. "But don't you forget, he's just a boy. And this is all new to him."

He nodded and kissed her on the cheek. "See you tonight."

David waited on the sidewalk, hopping uncontrollably. The dusting of snow glittered and crunched with every new footstep. He took Papa's hand as they passed the Jeffersons' house, half expecting Nellie to bolt from the bushes. But she was fast asleep on the back porch, dreaming of squirrels. And anyway, she wouldn't dare chase him with Papa there. His father was the strongest man in the world.

Allen looked down at his son, watching him lengthen his stride to stay in step. *Always trying to keep up*, he thought. *That's how it is when you're the youngest.*

"Papa, we're not late, are we?" David looked up with worry in his eyes.

"Late?!" Allen chuckled. "I wouldn't make a very good train man if I was late, would I?"

David grinned and shook his head.

They soon arrived at the train stop. The sky overhead was still dark, but the horizon whispered a rumor of dawn. David searched the inbound track for the glimmer of a headlight. For him, trains were better than fireworks and baseball and a new

Flexible Flyer all rolled into one. But he had never ridden on a train. Until today.

A silent point of light appeared and grew from a flicker to a beam. A low rumble rolled down the track bed, pierced by a whistle blast at the uptown crossing. David felt the train in his heart as the clanking, hissing, muscular hulk eased to a stop, exhaling its coal-scented breath.

"Wow," David puffed, and the word hung in the air and mingled with steam.

The conductor swung off the end of the steps and nearly landed on David.

"Whoa! Morning, Allen! And who might this young fella be?"

"Morning, Ted. This is my son David."

"Hello, David." The conductor stuck out his hand. "So you're riding along with your pa today, is that it?"

David looked down at his boots and nodded. Then a gentle nudge from Papa reminded him of Mama's last instructions, and he looked up at the conductor and shook his hand. "Yes, sir."

"Well, come on then — we got a schedule to keep." And he boosted David up onto the steps. Ted hit the signal bell twice for all clear, and the train lumbered forward.

"What line you got today?" Ted asked Papa.

"Bethlehem." Papa reached for his wallet. "Let me have round trip for the boy."

Ted frowned. "Put that away, Allen. Ain't nobody here except us three, what's he need a ticket for?"

"It's his first train ride, Ted. He'll want something to remember it by."

David opened his mouth to say that he would remember it even without a ticket. What stopped him was knowing that Papa would never take a thing for free that was meant to be paid for.

Ted reluctantly punched holes in the ticket and handed it to David. "Put it in your pocket, son."

Papa led the way down the aisle as the train picked up speed. Its rhythmic motion left David bouncing and stumbling along behind, until he slid into the seat and next to the window. He watched the town slip away in a blur, then the lumberyard, then a long stretch of fields.

"Papa, how fast are we going? As fast as Uncle Rudy's car?"

Papa considered for a moment, then said, "Right now I imagine we're going quite a bit faster than that. But you'll see when we go through towns that we slow down a lot."

David's wide eyes took everything in. As they approached the city, all the buildings squeezed closer together and stretched as far as David could see through the grimy window. Their pace slowed to a crawl, and David saw lines of trains on parallel tracks. Soon they inched into a huge building, and the train stopped with a loud hiss.

Papa stood up. "This is Reading Terminal. It's a big train station, one of the biggest. Come on. Stay close to me."

David reached for his father's hand. The station was like a machine with a hundred moving parts. The shoeshine man's hands gripped the cloth and became a blur of polishing, while his customer, in suit and tie, sat motionless behind a newspaper and a small cloud of cigarette smoke. All the stools were full at the lunch counter, where a generously-lipsticked waitress poured coffee, took orders, and delivered eggs and banter. The newsstand busily exchanged papers for pennies, and people bearing the weight of urgent business lined up at Western Union. Carrying duffel bags the size of small children, soldiers with home in their eyes consulted schedules and stood at attention in front of the ticket counter.

Through this kaleidoscope of activity, David trotted to keep up with Papa. They had nearly reached the gate when, from behind a big column, a young boy stepped into their path.

"Hey mister, you got any extra change?"

Papa stopped. The boy looked to be a few years older than David, but his coat was several sizes too big, dirty and torn. He tried not to shiver as he waited for Papa's response, and his eyes scanned the station quickly, like a rabbit alert for danger.

A string of thoughts circled Allen's mind and came to rest. He bent down. "Look at me, son," he said gently. "What's your name?"

A tug-of-war between hope and fear reflected in the boy's eyes.

"Jack," he said, edging backwards.

"Jack, I bet you're hungry. You wait here. I'm going to get you a sandwich." Allen took off his red scarf and handed it to the boy. "Here. You keep this."

Papa strode back to the lunch counter. David ran clumsily along beside, looking over his shoulder the whole time to watch the boy eagerly wrap the scarf around his neck.

"Papa," David began, "Why did that boy ask you for money? And why did you give him your scarf? And why..."

"Hush," Papa said. "I will explain it to you tonight on the train."

In a few minutes the waitress returned with two ham and cheese sandwiches in a paper bag. Papa and David re-crossed the station to where Jack waited in the shadows.

Papa handed the bag to Jack, and he reached inside immediately.

"Thanks, mister," he said, turning away.

Papa caught him by the shoulder and the boy flinched, as if by instinct. But then he realized that the man's grip meant no harm, and he turned back to Papa.

"Jack, I want to help you. I come to the station almost every day. I'll look for you again."

He let go, and the boy darted out the nearest exit.

Papa took David's hand and led him through the gate. He pointed to the waiting train — several passenger cars linked to an engine at the far end. "That's our train for today." He winked at David and added, "Maybe later we can go visit the engineer and fireman up front."

David settled down in a seat just inside the door of one of the cars. He watched the railroad men at work outside. Soon he heard Papa call "All aboard!" and the train hissed and lurched forward. "Service to Bethlehem! Stops at Lansdale, Souderton, Quakertown, Coopersburg, Hellertown. Tickets, please!" Papa moved down the aisle, from one car to the next, punching tickets and taking money.

After lunch, they had a short layover at the station. Papa and David walked along the platform to the front of the train. The engineer looked down at them from his window. "You better put that boy to work, Allen!" he yelled. "Frankie here could use a hand shovelin' coal." Papa helped David climb up into the engine. He stared at Frankie, who was covered with coal dust and sweat.

"Where's your shovel, boy?!" he asked with a loud laugh. The fire box sent out waves of heat, and David edged closer to Papa.

"Here, we still got a few minutes," the engineer said, motioning to David. "Lemme show you how to run this engine." He lifted David up onto the engineer's seat and put his hand on the throttle. "See... faster is this way... and slower is like this. Now here's the brake — you pull on it real hard. Takes a good long time to stop a train. And all these here dials, that's to tell you things about pressure and heat and so forth." David looked out the windshield and imagined flying down the track.

"OK, David, time to go," Papa said. "Tell the men thank you." David hopped down with a grin. "Thank you!"

"Thanks, fellas," Papa said. "And have a Merry Christmas."

The train made its last run of the day and pulled into the terminal. Papa showed David how to read the schedules and signs to find the train that would take them back home. They went on board and watched as the sun set and the city slipped away behind them. David suddenly felt very tired. He leaned against Papa and almost dozed off. Then he remembered.

"Papa?" he said. "What about that boy?"

Papa took a deep breath and let it out slowly. "That boy, I

believe, hasn't got anyone to care for him. And so he asks people in the station for money, so he can get something to eat."

"But what about his mama and papa?"

"Well, I don't know. It could be that something happened to them and he doesn't have other relations to take him in."

David considered this. "Where does he live, though?"

Papa didn't answer. He just looked out the window, into the darkness.

"Papa? Where does the boy live?"

Papa put his arm around David. "I don't know, son."

⊱——⊰

When they got home, David ran up the steps and opened the back door. The warm smell of gingerbread and the sound of Mama and his sisters rushed out into the night. In all the excitement of the train, he had almost forgotten that tomorrow was Christmas Day... but his brothers and sisters hadn't. It was all David could do to stay awake during supper. When he finished eating, Papa told him to go straight up to bed. And for once, David didn't wish he could stay up longer.

Eventually, the house grew quiet. Decorations were hung, the radio was turned off, and Papa added coal to the stove. He sat down on the sofa. Mama brought two cups of tea from the kitchen and sat down next to him.

"Allen, what happened today? Ever since you got back, it looks like your mind is somewhere else."

Allen held the steaming mug in both hands. "You're right, Annie. But I knew I couldn't tell you till later." He started at the beginning and told her about Jack.

Annie listened quietly. After he had finished, she said, "You want to help this boy."

There was a long silence, broken only by the ticking of the mantle clock and a few crackles from the stove. Then Allen looked up, and took Annie's hand.

"That could have been me," he said softly. "If it hadn't been for Uncle Dave and Aunt Helen... what would have become of me?"

Annie understood. Though he never spoke of it, she knew that every day he carried this in his heart. A gift that he lived his life to repay.

She squeezed his hand and nodded. "I'm with you in this." When she smiled, a few tears spilled onto her cheeks.

Allen gently brushed them away. "I don't know if I will see that boy again."

"God sees," Annie said.

The muffled words drifted up through the iron grate, to the room where a young boy slept, warm and safe between his brothers. The crescent moon shone through the frosty window... and also through a broken window in an abandoned shed, where a boy wrapped in a red scarf huddled against the cold and dreamed of seeing that man again.

LETTER

Beams of late afternoon sun created a mosaic of golden light and deep shadow throughout the town. The fullness of harvest time hung in the air — drying fruit and herbs and fish. The warmth of day would soon give way to the clear chill of night.

From the shadow of an alley, a young man emerged with energetic strides, tempered by a limp. As he turned down the main road, a glimpse of dark hair and a short beard was visible under the hood of his ordinary cloak. He carried a small bundle tucked under one arm and gripped a walking stick with the other hand.

Just past the Roman garrison, the man turned into a side street, out of reach of the last rays of the sun. He followed the pathway for a short distance, soon catching sight of a familiar building up ahead.

A narrow staircase at the side of the house led to a small upstairs room. The man climbed the stairs with difficulty and looked in at the window. By the light of an oil lamp, an old man set out his supper. His face instantly lit up with recognition and joy at the sound of a knock.

"Justus! Come in! My supper was only lacking someone to share it with, and here you are! I hoped you would come tonight."

"Hello, Doctor." After a quick embrace, the young man unwrapped his bundle and added fresh figs and olives to the table. The old man poured Justus a cup of wine. He took a loaf of bread in his hands, spoke a blessing, then broke it apart and gave half to Justus.

"How is your leg feeling?" the old man asked.

"A little better," Justus replied. "The wound still aches when I walk. The medicine you gave last time helps."

The old man nodded. "You also have youth on your side, which is the best medicine!" He chuckled. "But impossible to dispense."

It was a simple meal, enjoyed like a feast. Food and conversation were savored in equal measure, until there was not a crumb or a drop left. The lamp flickered gently, and soft noises of the night accompanied a comfortable pause.

Justus sensed his friend's weariness, an aging body in the grasp of an irrepressible spirit and an unfinished task. "You look tired. Will you continue the letter tonight?"

The old doctor didn't answer right away, and Justus studied his strong and gentle hands. They bore the scars of many journeys, and the blessing of a healing touch.

"I saw many of the sick today," the old man finally replied. "It takes a toll. But all day one thing kept pushing into my mind." He looked up at Justus. "I do want to continue tonight — will you write for me again?"

"Of course!"

Justus cleared the table. From a battered wooden box, the doctor brought out the letter, along with ink and several pens. Justus took his seat, adjusted the lamp, and chose a pen. At the edge of the circle of light, the old man settled into a chair, collecting his thoughts with a deep breath.

Pen poised, Justus waited. He glanced at the beginning of the letter...

Dear Theophilus,

… I have decided, since I have traced the course of these happenings carefully from the beginning, to set them down for you myself in their proper order, so that you may have reliable information…

Justus pictured the manuscripts the doctor had studied with a careful eye, their contents now stored in his razor-sharp mind. And all the people he had traveled miles to visit, their memories now as vivid as if they were his own.

The old man cleared his throat. He spoke slowly and thoughtfully. Sentence by sentence, the story unfolded…

"At that time a proclamation was made by Caesar Augustus that all the inhabited world should be registered. This was the first census, undertaken while Cyrenius was governor of Syria; and everybody went to the town of his birth to be registered."

"Excuse me. Cy – who?" Justus asked.

"Cyrenius. C-y-r-e-n-i-u-s."

"Joseph went up from the town of Nazareth in Galilee to David's town, Bethlehem, in Judea, because he was a direct descendant of David, to be registered with his future wife, Mary, who was pregnant.

"So it happened that while they were there in Bethlehem, she came to the end of her time. She gave birth to her first child, a son. And as there was no place for them inside the inn, she wrapped him up and laid him in a manger."

The old man paused, and Justus raised an eyebrow.

"Did you say a *manger?*"

"Yes." The scratching of the pen continued.

"There were some shepherds living in the same part of the country, keeping guard throughout the night over their flocks in the open fields. Suddenly an angel of the Lord stood before them, the splendor of the Lord blazed around them, and they were terrified. But the angel said to them, *Do not be afraid! Listen, I bring you glorious news of great joy which is for all the people. This very day, in David's town, a Savior has been born for you. He is Christ, the Lord. Let this prove it to you: you will find a baby, wrapped up and lying in a manger.*

"And in a flash there appeared with the angel a vast host of the armies of Heaven, praising God, saying, *Glory to God in the highest Heaven! Peace upon earth among men of goodwill!*"

The sound of the pen had stopped. Puzzled, the doctor paused and looked over at Justus. He was wide-eyed with wonder, pen suspended in mid-stroke.

"Oh! Sorry!" He carefully added the missing lines, and the old man continued.

"When the angels left them and went back into Heaven, the shepherds said to each other, *Now let us go straight to Bethlehem and see this thing which the Lord has made known to us.*

"So they went as fast as they could and they found Mary and Joseph — and the baby lying in the manger. And when they had seen this sight, they told everybody what had been said to them about the little child. And those who heard them were amazed at what the shepherds said."

The doctor paused, and Justus almost put down the pen. It sounded like the end of the story. But the old man gazed into the shadows, as if he saw a dear friend approaching in the distance.

"But Mary treasured all these things and turned them over in her mind. The shepherds went back to work, glorifying and praising God for everything that they had heard and seen, which had happened just as they had been told."

Now it was finished. The pen was silent. Justus stared at the words on the page. When he finally looked over at the doctor, the old man's eyes were closed and his shoulders sagged. Justus gently helped him into bed. He waited for the ink to dry, then carefully placed everything back into the wooden box. He closed the lid and secured the tiny latch.

As he returned the box to its shelf, Justus thought of the rest of the letter. Much of it was in his own handwriting, capturing the doctor's words from the air and fixing them onto the paper.

But somehow the words wouldn't stay on the paper. They got up and followed Justus around from morning to night. He felt them coming to life inside his heart, even as he went down the steps and limped home in the moonlight.

Made in the USA
Lexington, KY
06 May 2017